THE DARK FOREST

HEROES OF MEADOW HAVEN

BOOK I

DAVID A. BROGDON

Printed in the United States of America
First Printing 2015

Lightstone Publishing
ISBN-13: 978-0692558829
ISBN-10: 0692558829

Author Blog
learningtowrite87.blogspot.com

Cover Illustration created by Keith Draws
http://keithdraws.wordpress.com

ACKNOWLEDGEMENTS

I thank my maker for the beautiful gift of the written word, which allows me to create whatsoever I dream.

DEDICATION

I dedicate this book to my wife, Alyssa. You have always supported me, no matter what. I wouldn't be the person I am today if not for your love, loyalty, and friendship.

Chapter I

Roki dropped into a crouching position and silently snuck up through the tall brush next to Dax, who was peering over the hilltop into the distance.

"There it is!" Dax whispered over his shoulder.

Roki slowly lifted his head above the tall grass and peered over the hilltop at the scene before him. About 300 feet in front of them, down the hillside, was a flat clearing. Four ugly, green-skinned goblins surrounded a camp fire, grunting and speaking in Tarnak, or as most people called it, 'Goblin Tongue'. Over the fire, a large chunk of charcoaled meat was roasting. Roki could smell the warm, tender meat cooking and it made his stomach growl. Maybe eating breakfast would've been a good idea after all, he thought. One of the goblins sat on a heavy-looking log with a crude metal battle axe in hand. He sharpened it sloppily on a heavy stone as two other goblins stood across from each other, bantering, with axes in hand. The fourth goblin lazily tossed a few chunks of wood onto the large campfire.

Roki glanced over at Leena who was already halfway up a large tree, crouched on a branch, waiting for the go ahead to move in. Roki then looked to Dax, anticipating the orders. Dax stared at the camp for several moments, studying the layout and formulating his strategy. After a minute or two, Dax motioned for Leena to move in. Roki watched as she effortlessly glided and scaled along the tree top branches high overhead. She was not only quick, but completely silent.

After a few moments of bouncing from branch to branch, Leena came to rest almost directly above the four goblins. Roki checked the bandits for any sign that they had been alerted to her position. They hadn't noticed. The ugly creatures continued grunting and uttering nonsense, completely unaware of the danger that lurked above them. He looked at Dax, who now looked back at him intently. Dax didn't speak a word but Roki knew what he was waiting for. Roki shot a quick nod back to signify that he was ready to move forward.

Roki watched Dax as he began moving slowly through the tall weeds towards the camp, being sure to stay low into the grass to avoid detection. After a few seconds, Roki quietly circled out about 100 feet and began closing in from his own direction. He could feel his heart began to beat faster with anticipation of the battle before them. He had never fought a goblin, but he knew that they weren't generally regarded as particularly skilled fighters. Still, the three of them were outnumbered so it would pay to be cautious.

From previous battles he knew that a fight rarely went the way that it was expected to go. On any given day a battle could turn out differently than it would have the day before. He knew that he had to be ready. He wasn't going to be the weakest link or the one responsible for letting the goblins get the better of them.

Roki came to the spot where he felt he had an advantage and stopped, waiting for Dax to make the first move. Crouching down low, Roki listened to the loud clanging of the axe against the grindstone, and the grunting and huffing of the ugly creatures as they conversed in the foul sounding barbaric language. They sounded more like they were growling at each other rather than talking.

Roki peeked up slowly over the tall grass and across the clearing, towards Dax's direction, watching as his friend moved quietly and slowly into position. He then glanced up towards the tree branches to check one last time if Leena was ready. The thick, green leaves, and the fact that she was extremely cunning, made her nearly impossible to locate. Her movements were always hard to track, especially when she didn't want to be seen. Roki searched the twisted branches and vines before finally locating his almost invisible friend. She was tucked into a dark crevice, blanketed in a shadow with an arrow ready to fire. His anxious heart thumped in his chest.

All at once Dax exploded out of the thick brush towards the goblin bandits. He rushed fifty or so feet before the goblins were even alerted to his presence. Immediately they let out a fierce roar and charged towards him. The goblin that had been feeding the fire was a bit behind his comrades. As he reached down to grab his heavy steel mace Leena fired two arrows in rapid succession. *THWAP. THWAP.* Before the goblin could react, the arrows hit their mark. The first one slammed into the creature's side, causing it to let out only a split-second squeal before the second arrow sliced through its thick neck. The well-placed arrow silenced the ugly goblin instantly as his nearly lifeless body dropped like a bag of heavy rocks.

The three others hadn't even noticed their comrade's quick demise as they charged forward towards their target. Dax slowed to a jog and braced for the encounter. Roki looked ahead as the three goblins closed in on his friend. Dax was outnumbered. Roki lunged forward with incredible haste, putting all of his strength into a mighty swing with his hammer.

The swing collided with one of the goblins, sending him crashing into the goblin next to him. Both went rolling off into the tall brush. Roki got ready for their attack. Dax jumped back as the front goblin closed in and swung down hard with his heavy battle axe. The axe missed Dax's body by a few inches and slammed into the ground with a large crash.

Dax lunged forward, slicing through the air with his sharp blade. At the last moment the big goblin managed to raise his axe blade just high enough to deflect the attack, sending the creature stumbling backwards. One of the two goblins emerged from the brush in front of Roki, with an obvious vendetta against the one who landed the heavy hammer blow.

The goblin snarled loudly, contorting its face in an even uglier manner than its natural configuration, as it jumped at him with a mighty swing of its heavy axe. Roki side-stepped the vicious attack and rammed the goblin hard with his shoulder, staggering it backwards. He quickly followed up with spinning swing attack with his heavy hammer. The attack was off by a degree, hitting the goblin hard in the shoulder and sending it spinning into the ground. He raised his hammer high to finish the goblin, but as he was about to bring it down he heard a loud battle cry behind him.

He swung around quickly anticipating the impact of the goblins sharp axe. There was no time to react. Just as he was sure the attacker's swing would be successful, the charging goblin let out a high-pitched squeal as the hidden Leena dropped from the tree branches above, sinking her twin daggers into the unsuspecting creature's back.

It dropped with a loud thud and slid the last foot or so before stopping at Roki's feet. He quickly spun around to confront the other downed goblin. It had gotten up and now charged full speed towards Dax, who had his back turned as he had just finished pulling his now blue-colored blade from the chest of his first attacker.

Roki knew there was no time to react. He would never be able to reach the creature in time. Without thinking about it, he launched his heavy steel hammer forward with all his might, sending it hurling through the air towards the goblin. The hammer struck hard into the goblin's side, sending it flying into the trees. Dax turned around quickly but before he could engage the creature Leena had already fired several arrows. *THWAP. THWAP. THWAP.*

The goblin hadn't even stopped moving from the force of Roki's attack when the arrows slammed into their targets. The first two arrows pierced through the goblin's right and left shoulders pinning it to the tree behind it. The third arrow whizzed close behind, slamming hard into the creature's head with a loud crack. Dax stood there for a moment as the creature's lifeless body failed to drop to the ground due to the force at which the arrows had impacted into the tree, holding the three-hundred-pound goblin firmly in place. Roki looked around quickly in every direction. His heart thumped hard in his chest but began to slow down as he noticed all four of the goblins were now dead. Hopefully there weren't any more nearby.

Chapter II

After catching his breath for a moment, Roki began checking the goblins for any valuable loot. Dax took on the unappealing work of rounding up the goblin ears to exchange for the bounty reward. Once Leena had retrieved her arrows, she stood watch as they continued to work.

Roki looked down in front of him at the ugly goblin that lay motionless at his feet. Long jagged teeth shot up out of its mouth from its bottom jaw. A thick black patch of hair sat atop its green-skinned head. He reached down into the creature's leather vest pocket and pulled out a small handful of bronze coins and meaningless trinkets. He looked them over and shoved them into his belt pouch as he started towards the next goblin corpse.

Once Dax finished gathering the ears, he joined Roki in searching the bodies. Most of the loot was worthless stones and charms, with another small handful of bronze coins. After they had checked the last goblin, Roki and Dax stood up and made their way over to where Leena stood watch. As they closed in, Dax let out a relieved sigh.

"That was intense," he said.

Roki could still feel his heart beating a little faster than normal. It had been quite intense, but he had prepared for the worst. He was relieved that it had gone as smoothly as it had.

"It would have been a lot harder if not for Leena's well-placed arrows," Roki answered.

Leena returned a smile.

"Well, just remember, I may not always be around to watch your backsides!" Leena replied.

With her quip, Dax let out a laugh.

"Don't feed her ego, Roki."

Leena returned a scowl.

"Don't be jealous, Dax. It doesn't suit you," she said.

Dax laughed again and turned back towards the way they had come.

"I suppose we should head back now. It will be getting dark soon," Dax said, looking back at them.

Roki looked up at the mostly hidden blue sky above. He could still see a few spots of bright light, but he could tell that it was getting dimmer. They didn't want to get stuck in that part of the forest at night. Roki gave a quick nod at Dax, signaling that he was ready. Dax turned back around and began moving. Roki quickly fell into position, waiting for Leena to follow. He expected to hear her light footsteps coming up behind him, but after a few feet he stopped and looked back. She hadn't moved from her spot. He narrowed his eyes, confused, and watched as Leena stood there motionless with an odd look on her face. Her eyes met his with a quick but calm glance to let him know everything was okay. She seemed to be listening to something.

Roki slowed his somewhat heavy breathing and concentrated, in an effort to pick up on the sound. He didn't hear anything at all, apart from the normal deep forest sounds. He slowly and silently moved a little closer to where Leena was standing. He focused harder and listened. He could hear the faint whistling of the wind in the tree limbs high above. He could hear his own heart thumping in his chest. *CLANK*. There it was. A sound so quiet and muffled that it almost couldn't be heard.

He looked back at Dax, who had quickly figured out what they were doing and now crept slowly up behind them. Leena pointed towards a very large tree stump about fifteen feet away. It was easily five or six feet wide and had leaves and brush growing up the sides.

Roki and the others quietly made their way over to the stump to investigate. Without hesitation, Dax leaned over and peered down into the large hole. His eyes widened as a surprised look formed on his face. Dax motioned quickly for the others to join him. As Roki leaned over and peered down into the dark stump, he couldn't believe his eyes. Two or three feet down, about ground level, a wooden hatch lay open. Beneath the hatch was a wooden ladder leading straight down into a dark passage. He couldn't see the bottom. What had they stumbled onto?

Roki looked over at Dax and Leena as the two studied each other's faces for a moment. It only took a second or two for Dax and Leena to silently agree on descending into the passage. They then turned and looked at him, waiting for his response.

As Roki stared down into the dark below, he couldn't help but feel uneasy about it. There was no way to know where it would lead them, or what might be waiting for them down below. He wasn't scared, he just wasn't a fool either. He always tried to think ahead about what could happen in any given situation. He liked to plan for the worst possible outcome. As dedicated as he was, sometimes his friends' decisions left him feeling reluctant.

After a moment of contemplation, he looked back at his two eager friends and gave the signal that he was in. Dax nodded back with a faint smile, climbed over the stump, and began moving down the rickety wooden ladder into the passage below. After a few seconds, both Dax and Leena had disappeared down into the passage. Roki took once last glance around at the silent forest and started climbing down the ladder.

Roki dropped the last two or three feet onto the rocky ground beneath. He bent his knees to absorb the shock from the fall and to keep from making a loud noise as his heavy boots hit the ground. Dax and Leena were already standing in front of him, peering down the dark corridor ahead.

The corridor was built of mostly square, grey stones, with patches of brown, clay dirt showing here and there. It extended about fifty feet ahead and then turned off to the left. It would've been completely dark if not for the occasional dimly-lit torch fastened securely to the stone walls on either side.

The corridor was just wide enough for them to fall into defensive positions. Dax took the lead as usual, with Leena off to his left to cover flank. Roki assumed his position just off to Dax's right side. The three of them shot a quick glance at each other and quietly began down the path. They hadn't walked ten feet when the sound of heavy footsteps caught their ears. Roki raised his large hammer and looked over at Dax, who was already perched. Leena had her bow at full draw, and sat crouched against the left wall in a shadow, ready to fire.

After a few seconds the large shape of a goblin scout rounded the corner. It stopped in its tracks just a foot or two after rounding the corner as its eyes widened with the sight of the three adventurers. Leena snapped the bowstring quickly, firing off an arrow.

Before the goblin could sound off, Leena's arrow met its mark with perfect accuracy, piercing the creature's throat. The arrow went almost completely through, changing its would-be war cry into a low gurgle. The large goblin took a step backwards and fell into the stone wall behind it, sliding down into a sitting position with its eyes closed. Dax waited for a moment to make sure it was dead before advancing past it and down the corridor.

He and Leena followed close behind, stepping over the lifeless goblin as they rounded the corner and began down the short hallway. In front of them was a sturdy wooden door that hung open. Roki watched ahead as Dax crept slowly through the door and into the room in front of him. Leena followed close behind.

As Roki passed the wooden doorway and walked into the large open room, he glanced around quickly. The room was empty besides a wooden table with a few scraps of paper strewn across it and a rickety wooden chair underneath. Two or three torches lined the walls of the room, casting at least a little light into the otherwise dark corners. Directly across from him was another heavy wooden door, though this one was closed, and off to the right was another dark corridor.

Dax looked back and motioned to the door. Roki and Leena nodded silently in agreement and watched as Dax lifted slowly on the sturdy iron handle, being careful to make the least amount of noise as possible. With a small creak, the door came open. They quickly moved through the doorway and into the dark hallway ahead. The dimly lit corridor extended for only a short way before dropping into a downward staircase. They quietly began moving down the stone steps and into the sub level. At the bottom of the steps, Roki stopped behind Leena as Dax peered around a corner to the left.

Roki could hear faint echoes and a loud grinding noise with an occasional clanking sound. He looked at Dax who signaled that there was danger ahead. Leena pulled back on the nocked arrow, nearly bringing it to full draw before nodding quickly at Dax to advance.

Roki followed close behind, with his hammer ready, as Dax and Leena shot around the corner all at once.

Immediately the goblin was alerted to the threat and let out a loud snarl. The raging goblin raised its battle axe high in the air and charged. As the goblin cleared the large, stone pillar that had prevented Leena's death shot, she snapped off an arrow quickly. *THAP.*

It collided hard with the goblin's weapon hand, sending his whole arm hurling backwards just as it was about to reach them. The heavy iron battle axe bounced loudly as it hit the stone floor. Before the creature could recover from the staggering shot, Dax rushed in, swiftly sinking his sharp steel sword into the goblin's chest. It let out a shriek, followed by a rough growl before dropping to the floor. As its lifeless body hit the ground, another goblin burst through a small wooden door off to the right.

With little time to react, Roki put everything he had into a huge swing of his heavy hammer. The goblin rushed forward as the steel hammer collided with the creature's chest plate, making a loud crashing sound. The goblin flew backwards and slammed into the heavy wooden door behind it, shattering it into large splinters. It fell to the ground, gasping for only a split-second before Leena's second arrow collided with its head, putting the creature out of its misery.

Roki waited for a second, expecting more attacks. After it was clear no other goblins were going to rush in, he lowered his hammer to his side and began looking around the dimly lit room. Heavy iron chains hung from iron rings attached to the stone walls. Dark red liquid stained the floor. It didn't take him long to realize it was some type of jail.

In front of them a few feet, was a large grindstone that the goblin had been using to sharpen his axe blade before they entered. Across from that was a wooden table with a few iron tools on it and some unlit torches. Roki quickly made his way over to the table and loaded the torches into his bag. He always liked to be as prepared as possible. There was no telling when they might need some extra light.

Dax and Leena quickly moved away from him in different directions, each searching the dark shadows of the room. At the back of the room he noticed three or four small jail cells, with heavy iron bars. The lack of a lit torch at the back of the room made it difficult to see inside. He pulled one of the wall torches free from its fixture and walked towards the dark cells. After a few paces, he stopped. An odd noise caught his attention. It was like a faint moaning.

Roki held the torch high out in front of him, struggling to see. As he got closer to the bars, the light from the torch illuminated the dark shadows ahead. He was instantly startled as the image caught him off-guard. Hanging from a set of rusty iron shackles was a frail and thin old man. The man's weak and brittle-looking body was covered only by a thin, stained undergarment. Fresh cuts and wounds peppered his bony arms and ribcage. A long, scraggly grey beard hung from his face. Roki waved with the torch to get Dax and Leena's attention and then motioned for them to come over. They closed in quickly behind him and stood in silence, staring at the frail prisoner. At last a quiet hoarse voice spoke.

"Help me," the man said.

"Please, get me out of here."

The old man started to sob. Roki looked at Dax and Leena, who still stared at the man.

"We can't just leave him chained down here," he said.

Dax looked back at him for a moment, contemplating.

"You're right, Roki, we can't. It wouldn't be right. Maybe one of those goblins was carrying a cell key."

At Dax's idea, Leena moved off quickly to search the goblin corpses. After a few moments, she returned to the cell with a rugged iron key in hand.

"This must be it," Leena said, handing the key to Roki.

He stuck the iron key into the lock without hesitation and turned it until the heavy iron gear clicked. As soon as it did, the heavy door swung open. Roki, being the cautious one, looked back at Dax for reassurance. Dax seemed to study his face for a moment before speaking.

"It's your call," Dax said.

Roki turned back and looked at the battered old man. His eyes were soft and kind. His body was frail and weak. How could he be any kind of threat? After making up his mind, Roki reached up and unlocked the heavy iron shackles that held up the man's arms. He pulled the iron pins from the cuffs and removed them from the man's wrists. The skin beneath was torn, raw, and bloody. Once loose, the old man immediately fell onto Roki. Roki grabbed him and set him softly down upon an old wooden bench that sat on the ground below the shackles. The man groaned loudly as the wounds on his side met the rough wooden boards.

"I will carry him out of here" Roki said to the others. Before Dax and Leena could respond, the old man interrupted.

"You have done enough, friends. I need to rest now," the frail man whispered.

Roki paused for a moment.

"Are you sure you can make it out of here alone?" Roki asked, hesitantly.

The old man struggled to speak again.

"I will be fine. Thank you. I will not forget this," he said.

With that, the man's head dropped to the wooden bench and his eyes closed. Roki let out a relieved sigh as the faint raising and lowering of the man's chest revealed that he was indeed still alive. He would need to rest.

"Let's at least cover him with something before we leave" Roki said quietly.

He glanced around the room for something to cover the poor man with. In the corner of the room, next to the jail cells, he spotted a rough woven flour sack. Roki grabbed the large sack and turned to cover the man, draping the thick cloth over the man's starved and battered body. As he exited the cell, he looked back one last time at the poor old man. He would've thought the man dead if it wasn't for the slightest movement of his ribcage up and down as he breathed. Hopefully, once he regained his strength, he would be able to make it out. Roki hated just leaving him there, but he wasn't going to force the man. It was his choice.

"Let's explore the rest of this place and get back to Meadow Haven," Dax said in a quiet voice.

Roki agreed and followed closely behind Dax and Leena as they headed back up the steps, through the door, and into the previous room. They entered the room slowly, with Dax peering around to check for danger. After a moment, Dax motioned behind him for them to follow. They moved to the left and headed down the dark corridor that was yet to be explored. Dimly-lit torches lined the walls like before but didn't seem to give much light.

After about fifty or sixty feet, the left wall opened into a large room. Roki could see the light casting shadows onto the stone wall directly across from the doorway. The corridor extended at least another thirty feet past the room on the left until it grew too dark for him to see down. He watched as Dax inched forward toward the room's opening pace by pace.

Dax's round shield was readied in his left hand and his sword drawn in his right. He watched as Dax shot a quick glance down the dark corridor ahead before turning his attention back to the well-lit room. Dax slid up next to the cold stone wall and peeked through the open doorway. His sword hand went up as he gave the signal that there was danger in the room.

Leena swung around next to him with her bow at full draw, ready to release an arrow. Roki looked into the room from behind Leena. It was a well-lit room with a stone floor. Along the edges of the room were five or six wooden weapon racks decorated with shiny axes and a few maces. Rugged goblin armor hung from iron hooks on the walls every few feet. Roki could see at the other end of the closed in room were probably twenty or more empty beds. In the center of the room at a long wooden table sat a goblin with his back to the doorway.

Just as Leena was about to release her bowstring, a large goblin appeared down the corridor walking towards them. There was nothing they could do to avoid detection. The goblin stopped dead in its tracks and let out a loud raging snarl. Roki knew that most goblins possessed significantly more brawn than brains, which should've led the goblin to attack the three of them without hesitation. But maybe this goblin had a small amount of intellect. Instead of charging recklessly forward at full speed, it turned around and started sounding a loud alert, as it disappeared back down the dark corridor.

The sitting goblin immediately jumped up and reached for the shiny axe that rested on the table in front on it. Before it could turn around, an arrow exploded from Leena's bow. It impacted hard into the goblins back causing it to let out a shriek. Another arrow followed right behind, slamming into its mark not even an inch above the first. This time the goblin didn't make a noise. Its large body convulsed slightly as it slumped forward onto the table in front of it. Roki watched as blue liquid quickly ran across the table and onto the floor. Dax quickly developed a frantic look on his face.

"We have to stop that goblin in case he alerts any others about us!" Dax said quickly, as he darted down the corridor after the fleeing goblin.

Roki followed Leena as she chased down the hallway after Dax. When they caught up to Dax he was standing still, looking down into a deep, square hole in the floor that was about five feet across. A large iron pulley was securely bolted into the stone ceiling, with a thick chain dropping down an unmeasurable distance into the dark hole.

"He took the lift down before I could catch him," said Dax, concernedly. "We have to stop him."

Roki knew Dax was right. If the goblin alerted others to their presence, the goblins might be able catch up to the three of them before they could make it out. It could be a bloodbath. Roki nodded to Dax understandingly and tossed him the long, brown rope that he had bought back in town.

"Tie that to the pulley," Roki instructed.

Dax tied the rope securely and tossed the rest down into the dark hole. Then Dax reached out with his thick leather gloves and grabbed onto the sturdy rope in front of him, dropping down into the hole with a whizzing sound. Leena shrugged slightly as she stared down at the hole, before dropping quickly down behind Dax. Roki tried not to think about what might be down there waiting for them. There was no turning back now. He reached out and latched onto the rope with his leather covered hands. Once his boots were wrapped tightly around the rope, he let his grip relax, sending him falling into the dark below.

Chapter III

Roki landed on top of the large wooden lift with a thud and leaped off onto the ground, bending his knees to absorb the impact. He turned to his friends who were already looking around at the magnificent scene before them. He couldn't help but let his jaw drop open as he observed the environment.

They had dropped into a massive cavern, carved from pure ebony. It seemed dark at first, but after a second he noticed large glowing crystals embedded in the walls of the cavern. They put forth a kind of artificial yellow light that made every detail of the cavern visible. Large natural pieces of the ceiling flowed down to the floor, creating pillar formations. The floor of the cavern was mostly flat with a few small piles of stone here and there. Large carts made of wood and banded together with iron littered the floor of the cavern. The wooden carts were filled with big chunks of the black rock, some of which contained pieces of the glowing crystals.

Roki paced forward, looking around the cavern. It was eerily silent. Not a movement. Not a stir. Not an echo. Leena was already scanning the room for signs of danger as Dax studied the terrain intensely. Roki didn't like the look of the place. Where was everyone? Surely somebody or something had done all that mining? The small number of goblins they had come across could not have mined the area by themselves. They had already seen what appeared to be the living quarters back inside the armory where all the beds were empty. So, where were they?

Dax found what seemed to be a pathway and began to follow it, motioning to the others to follow. Roki closed in behind Leena, who was aggressively searching every nook and cranny as she started to creep quietly along the path. As Roki walked, he slipped his right hand through the small loop at the end of his hammer. The leather strap looping around his wrist would give him more control over the weapon if he found himself in a situation where he needed to swing it aggressively.

The movements had cost him a couple paces, so he hurried ahead to fall in close behind Leena again. As they advanced further in to the cavern the ceiling and walls got more and more narrow, creating a long corridor around them. The corridor was littered with bright glowing crystals which created a luminous glow all around.

The corridor was too narrow to stay in formation, so he fell in behind Leena as she moved in directly behind Dax. As he walked, Roki tried not to let the dreamy glow of the yellow crystals distract him, but the cool air and the soft pulsing yellow light against the black ebony stone made it difficult to stay focused. After a lengthy trek through the narrow tunnel, it finally opened back out into another large cavern much like the one they had come from.

As Roki exited the corridor into the large cavern, he moved back out a few paces to the right of Dax to get a good look. The path in front of them sloped steeply downwards for twenty or thirty feet before flattening out into a large, flat area. Huge rock structures shot up from the ground here and there and large pillars reached from floor to ceiling. In the distance ahead, past the clearing, he could see a large doorway cut out of the rock, with a heavy iron door leading into another area.

Roki quickly got Dax and Leena's attention and motioned towards the door. Dax studied it for a moment before he gave the signal to advance. The three of them crouched down low and walked as softly as possible, hoping to catch whatever was in the other room by surprise. They paced forward down the steep hill until they reached the bottom and got ready to advance into the clearing.

As they moved forward, Dax suddenly spotted the goblin that had retreated from them earlier. As Dax motioned behind him to get their attention, the goblin let out a loud snarl and disappeared behind a large rock formation ahead. Roki looked at Dax, whose face crinkled with rage as he took off charging toward the goblin.

"Noooo!" Roki cried out, trying to stop Dax's advance.

He knew exactly what was going on. That goblin had led them to the cavern for a reason. He wasn't fleeing for his life. He wasn't hiding from them. He was a smart goblin, a crafty one. But it was too late and Roki knew it. He couldn't warn Dax fast enough. There was no choice left.

Roki charged after his friend with a furious haste. He had to be there to protect his friend. He got close to Dax as Dax entered the middle of the clearing. "Dax, stop!" Roki cried loudly. This time Dax heard his friend's voice. But it was too late. Loud screams rattled the cavern as hordes of goblins poured out from behind the large rock structures surrounding the clearing. It was exactly as he had feared. It was an ambush... and there was no retreat.

Roki looked around in awe as the goblins poured down the sides of the cavern towards them. He didn't like the odds. There had to be twenty, maybe thirty, goblins surrounding them, with some on every side. And where was Leena? He shot a quick glance behind them. She was nowhere in sight. He didn't see her anywhere and he didn't have time search.

Roki turned around just in time to see the first group of goblins collide with Dax's shield. To his right, another small group lunged towards him. He swung his hammer with all his strength crashing into the two goblins in the front of the pack, sending the entire group flying backwards.

He brought the heavy hammer back with both hands and shot a quick glance at Dax. Dax's shield was just deflecting a crushing blow as his sword slid out of the chest of another attacker, sending blue liquid spraying onto the floor. The bloodied goblin fell to the ground, landing atop another fallen enemy that had already met Dax's blade. Roki turned back around to meet his next attackers. One goblin out in front of the pack lunged at him, bringing down its sharp axe with a mighty swing. Roki jumped hard to his right, dodging the attack, and quickly followed up with a strong swing of his hammer into the creature's side. The blow crushed the creature's ribcage instantly and sent it flying backwards into the group.

Roki swung around behind him with a quick thrust of his hammer, sending it slamming into another goblin's skull. A quick glance at Dax eased his nerves a bit. Dax was having no problem holding his own, as usual. He watched as Dax spun around quickly, swinging his sword hard into the attacker's leg. The blade sliced nearly all the way through the goblin leg with ease, causing it to let out a loud painful cry.

Dax quickly followed up with another attack, his sharp blade piercing its chest and ending its quest for vengeance. Another axe blade deflected off Dax's shield as he sunk his blade into his next foe. He was good. But Roki knew that they were still grossly outnumbered, and the horde was closing in on them more and more each second. The odds weren't very good.

Roki landed another blow as his hammer crashed into the chest of the next lunging goblin, sending it tumbling backwards into the others. Turning to his left, he put all his strength into hurling his heavy steel hammer forward into a wave of advancing goblins. The hammer slammed into the group with a large crash, causing the goblins to tumble back into the ranks behind them. With such a heavy impact, it didn't surprise him that a few of the goblins didn't get back up.

Roki lunged forward, anxious to capitalize on the successful attack. He snatched the hammer up with both arms and immediately put his full weight into another monstrous swing. The steel collided hard with another goblin, immediately crushing every bone in its large chest. The impact sent the creature flipping into the crowd with a gasping shriek. Roki took a step back and cracked another attacker in the face with the hammer's blunt wooden handle.

The blow crushed the goblin's nose in, causing it to swing its axe blindly in pain. He quickly ducked the wild attack and planted his heavy hammer firmly into the side of the goblin's head. The green-skinned skull exploded like glass, sending blue blood spraying everywhere. Roki quickly glanced around. Despite his and Dax's excellent fighting, they were still surrounded. More and more kept pouring in from all sides. There were just too many. Roki looked over at Dax who was still moving as quickly as ever, dropping goblin after goblin. Dax would go on forever, but Roki's arms were starting to get tired from swinging the heavy hammer swing after swing. He was getting tired, but he couldn't give up.

He turned around and placed his back against Dax's, readying himself for the final wave of goblins that had now completely encircled them. It was no longer multiple small groups. The rest of the ugly creatures moved towards them as one unit, shoulder to shoulder. The goblin horde charged ahead with a furious battle cry. Roki tried to prepare himself for the grizzly battle he was about to face. He felt his hands clench down tightly on the hard handle of his hammer.

Just as the raging creatures closed in, a familiar sound rang out. *THWAP. THWAP. THWAP. THWAP.* Roki flinched from the warm liquid that sprayed across his face as Leena's first arrow collided with the head of a goblin off to his left. Its heavy lifeless body dropped hard to the ground, sending a few goblins tripping forward. More arrows flew with perfect accuracy, piercing the thick skulls of specially selected targets across the battlefield.

Roki felt a smile force itself onto his face. Finally, they had some backup. He charged forward with renewed courage towards the advancing creatures. He could hear Leena's bow rapid-firing a multitude of arrows down upon the goblin horde. He could hear bodies dropping every second as the hurling arrows collided into their targets. It seemed that Leena had predicted the ambush even earlier than he had, and worked to get a good vantage point to mount an attack.

Roki slammed his hammer hard into his next attacker. Then another growling goblin met the crushing steel of his hammer. A quick-shot glance behind him revealed Dax dodging and weaving, around and under axe blades, exploiting his enemies' defensive weaknesses with the utmost aggression and precision.

Roki's hammer flew forward in front of him, colliding with the last goblin's legs. The powerful blow snapped its thick leg bones like twigs, causing it to let out an agonizing cry. The next strike came down hard on top of its skull, ending its misery. With throbbing arms, he lifted his heavy steel hammer once more and heaved it onto his shoulder. Deep pain shot down his right arm and into his shoulders and back. He turned to see his friends standing still, looking over the fallen goblin horde. Bodies littered the large cavern floor surrounding the three adventurers.

Roki breathed in deeply, trying to catch his breath and slow his heart rate. Pain shot from his forearms up his biceps on both arms. The heavy weapon had taken its toll on his body. His arms and shoulders were severely worn and swollen with damage. He painfully lifted his heavy hammer and slid the wooden handle through the holster that was secured to his back by leather straps.

Once his arms were free of the heavy weight, he instantly started to feel better. He took another deep breath and walked over to his friends. Leena was already retrieving her arrows from goblin corpses and Dax was pocketing whatever loot he could find. Roki quickly searched a few goblins as well, yielding more copper and a few jewels. Their adventure had become quite lucrative. After filling his small pouch with the coins and jewels, he walked over to Dax who was standing in front of the large metal door. Leena finished gathering her arrows and walked up next to them.

"The goblin that led us into that ambush disappeared through this door," Dax said.

Roki could tell by the look on his face that Dax was out for revenge. Dax turned to Leena who met his glance with a blank expression.

"Let's finish this, then," Leena said, readying her bow.

Roki added a fatigued nod as the weight of his own arms seemed to try and drag him down to the ground. Dax pulled hard on the heavy iron handle and the door swung open. He paced ahead with his sword drawn, Leena following close behind. Roki drew a small dagger from his boot. Since his arms were too weak to be accurate with his hammer, the dagger would have to do.

They passed through the door and immediately started to climb a steep set of stone steps. At the top, a short corridor curved around to the right and opened into a large, well-lit room. The stone walls were ornately decorated with hanging lanterns and stone archways. In the middle of the room was a large table decorated with ornate silver furnishings.

Large chunks of meat sat atop a silver platter in the middle of the table. In one corner was a large cabinet. Next to the cabinet was a small open chest with expensive animal furs hanging out onto the floor. Nearby, on the same wall, was a small table with precious jewels and various expensive pieces of jewelry. On the other side of the room were wooden crates, filled with grains, cured meats and other various foods. Next to the wooden crates, a glass case sat against the wall with a few old relics inside. The rest of the room was lined with equally impressive items.

Across the room from the entrance was a large bed with expensive fabrics draped over it. Roki had never seen such nice furnishings. He didn't expect them in a goblin hideout. The goblins had to have been operating out of the underground base for years. Dax walked along the edge of the room looking at the different objects.

"This must be the leader's quarters," Dax said.

"This is where all the loot goes that they pillage."

As Dax was still speaking Roki's attention snapped over to a large crash on the other side of the room. The nasty goblin that had plotted their demise busted out of the wooden cabinet that he had been hiding in and with one quick motion, hurled his shiny battle axe at full speed towards Dax. The axe sliced through the air in a spinning frenzy. Leena quickly drew back hard on her bow and released with only a split second to aim. The arrow exploded out of the wooden bow with a vengeance, whizzing straight towards the flying axe. The arrow collided with the axe on its mark, but it wasn't heavy enough to divert the attack away from Dax as Leena had hoped.

With no time for him to bring up his shield, the heavy axe collided with Dax's shoulder, sending him spinning off his feet. Leena turned quickly towards the attacker with another arrow ready, but he had already retreated up a steep set of stairs that Roki hadn't noticed before. As Leena looked back at Dax's bloody shoulder, Roki watched her facial expression change from concentration to pure hatred. He had never seen her show such hostility before. She was always so calm and collected, focused.

Almost without touching her feet to the floor Leena blazed forward and up the stairs, disappearing above. Roki quickly ran to Dax who had already gotten to his feet, thick red blood pouring from a large wound on his left shoulder. Dax somehow managed to still hold his shield in his left hand as he slid his shiny sword into its sheath. Just then an ungodly death shriek came from the top of the long steep staircase.

"LEENA!" he and Dax screamed simultaneously.

Roki threw his arm under Dax's ribcage and grabbed him hard, rushing forward. Dax grunted with agony as they bounced up each step quickly. As the two friends reached the top of the long staircase, and stepped outside, the scenery immediately changed from dark underground clay and rocks into the familiar green trees and grass of the forest. Roki let go of Dax and at the same time lifted up on the heavy hammer that hung from his back, drawing it into his hands.

His fear quickly faded into disbelief at the grizzly site before him. Leena stood in front of him, breathing heavily, with her bow fully drawn and ready to fire. On the ground, thirty or forty feet in front of her, was a large puddle of blue liquid, atop of which rested a mangled green object with more arrows sticking out of it than he cared to count.

He looked over at Leena's nearly empty quiver and then back down at the retired goblin. It was hard to see through the mess of arrow fletching to discern exactly what part of the goblin he was looking at.

After a moment of heavy breathing Leena finally relaxed her arm and let the arrow slide back down the bow limb into an undrawn position. She then turned and flashed a look at Roki that he had never seen before. It was a contrasting expression that revealed fear and courage, hatred and love. He could tell Leena had emotions that she hadn't allowed herself to fully understand yet. He could tell that she cared deeply for them both and would do anything to protect them, even at her own peril if necessary. He had always known that, but the look that he now saw in her eyes after she had destroyed the creature responsible for Dax's injury was something deeper, something he had never seen in her before. He wondered if she was even aware of her feelings. The look faded as Leena quickly moved over to Dax to inspect his injuries. As soon as she reached him she spoke in a slightly frantic tone

"How bad is it?" Leena questioned.

Dax had sheathed his sword and was kneeling on one knee, holding his wounded shoulder with his right hand. Red blood ran smoothly down his left arm as he grunted with pain.

"The wound is pretty deep," Dax answered, through clenched teeth. "I'll need to stop the bleeding somehow."

Roki thought about how far they had come from the entrance. It would take them nearly a day to reach a healer. They would have to make a temporary suture to try and stop the bleeding. Then he remembered about the herbs he had purchased back in Meadow Haven.

"Hold on a second," Roki said, rifling into his bag.

He pulled out the mangled mess of glittering green herbs and handed them to Dax.

"Here, I bought these back in town," Roki said.

Dax grabbed the bright green herbs and tossed them into his mouth. As he chewed on the wad of herbs, Roki couldn't help but feel glad that he wasn't the one having to eat them. He knew from previous experience that the texture was hard to chew, and the flavor was bitter. He hadn't had to use healing herbs in a long time, but it wasn't an easy taste to forget. After a few moments of chewing with a sour face, Dax finally swallowed the herbs and leaned back against a large grey rock that was directly behind him.

"It will take a little time for the herbs to work. I will need to rest for a bit" Dax said, as he dropped his head down and closed his eyes.

"Okay. I'll keep watch," Leena said, walking off a little way in the opposite direction.

Roki looked around, observing the area. The steep staircase had led them out of the underground goblin hideout and back into the forest above. Thick, overgrown trees surrounded and enclosed the small clearing that they now stood in. The grass beneath their feet was short, with light brown dirt showing through. Large branches covered in dark green leaves hung low, only a few feet above their heads.

Directly in front of Roki, a rugged path cut through a narrow opening in the trees. Leena was off to his left watching the tree line for signs of danger. The forest light had grown darker. Roki could still see quite a way in front of him but nightfall was closing in quickly.

Nearly half an hour passed by before Dax finally awoke and lifted his head. Hearing the movement, Roki quickly snapped around to see Leena already helping him to his feet.

"I'm okay," Dax said quickly.

Dax stood to his feet and looked over at his left shoulder to inspect his deep wound. Roki looked with amazement at the wound which had almost completely healed. All that remained was a small slice about two inches long and barely deep enough to sting. Dax slowly swung his left arm around in a circular motion a few times to check its mobility.

"It's fine. I'm ready to move," he said, as he turned to inspect the new area. Dax looked around in every direction.

"We should see what lies down that path," Dax said, pointing down a soft looking trail in the distance.

Leena looked over at the path and then at Roki. She seemed indifferent.

"It will be growing dark soon," Roki objected. "We have already sustained one injury today. Shouldn't we head back to Meadow Haven?"

Dax considered his words only for a moment before speaking.

"There is no way we will get back before nightfall. We will have to camp in the forest tonight regardless of if we head back now. Shouldn't we scope out the area before we set up camp? Besides, we have never been to this part of the forest before, aren't you two the least bit curious about what lies ahead?"

Roki looked at Leena who had a blank stare on her face as if she was waiting for them to finish the debate without her opinion. Then he looked back at Dax who had an eager look on his face as if his injury had never happened. Roki still felt reluctant, but before he could object again, Dax responded

"Let's just check out what's beyond this clearing. If it's safe, we'll explore a bit. If it looks questionable we'll head back here and set up camp," Dax said.

Roki looked back again at the narrow opening ahead of them. It looked soft and quiet. A pale glow illuminated the area around the opening, as if inviting them to enter. It didn't look dangerous at all actually.

After a moment of contemplation, he decided to indulge in Dax's adventurous outlook. Dax could tell immediately that he had persuaded his friend and drew his sword again into his right hand. Leena gave a quick confirmation and Dax quickly took the lead as they started down the rugged path through the narrow opening in the trees.

Chapter IV

This part of the forest was different than what Leena was used to. She watched ahead as they crept forward down the deep forest path. Large overgrown trees grew along either side of them with heavy foliage overhead. Long green vines grew down from above, wrapping around branches and down the large tree trunks.

It wasn't nearly as populated by creatures as the areas closer to the entrance. She carefully scanned the sides of the path for movement. She controlled her breathing and focused her eyes intently. Her ears were perked, listening for danger. She took the job of scout seriously. She knew that being born half wood elf gave her an advantage in the forest. Her special emerald-green eyes allowed her to see through the dark easier than the others. Her ability to focus her hearing allowed her to pick up sounds that they would often miss. It was her self-appointed duty to use her abilities to watch out for the team. She was happy to do it. She was good at it. It came as natural as breathing to her.

She looked ahead as Dax followed the rugged trail, his yellow-orange hair spiked forward and up at a sharp angle. His stance made him look ready, though much more confident than cautious. His slender yet muscular build showed his years of hard work and training. In his right hand he held his sword in a peculiar way with the blade turned slightly outwards away from his body. Watching him made her feel awkward. She was all about accuracy, focus, leverage. His form looked sloppy. He had a distinct style that, upon first viewing, would lead most to assume his skills were sub-par. But she knew that his fighting skills were anything but lacking.

Leena glanced back at Roki who was already looking at her. He always seemed to look at her periodically, searching for some sort of validation that she was comfortable with the situation. Compared to Dax's outlook, Roki was much more rigid. He always had a cautious look on his face and didn't seem nearly as confident as Dax. He had a wide build with a thick chest and large shoulders and arms. He held his large steel maul in both hands, his leather gloves gripped tightly around the handle. The heavy weight of the weapon made the veins bulge out of his arms as he carried it, making them look even stronger. She admired his strength and endurance, though she knew that his fighting skills could not match Dax's or her own. Even still, he was a worthy ally and had managed to hold his own in every battle they had faced. She was glad to have him watching her back.

As they advanced deeper into the forest, the path became more and more pronounced, with the density of the trees becoming much heavier. Eventually the trees and vines grew so dense that they started to form a nearly impenetrable wall, lining the path on either side. After quickly realizing that no creatures would be able to get through the dense trees to attack them, she turned her attention towards the forest ceiling that now rose into the darkness high above. She followed closely behind Dax looking up for any signs of movement or danger as he forged ahead down the path.

As they went on, she quickly realized that the forest had grown quite dark. She couldn't tell whether nightfall had set in or if the dense foliage had blocked out most of the remaining sunlight. A greyish white haze slowly began to creep up from the ground. Within minutes the haze had grown into a thick white fog, making it very hard to see even a few feet ahead. Dax came to a halt in front of her. The fog was making it difficult for him to advance any further. He paced forward another few feet and stopped again.

"I can't see," Dax said turning towards them.

"It has grown pretty dark in here and this fog is making it impossible to see what's ahead of us. It would be foolish to continue," Dax said.

Leena contemplated his words for a moment and responded.

"We should head back. We can save this exploration for another day," she said.

Roki gave a nod to show his agreement and they started back towards where they had come from. She moved quickly to catch up as Dax's pace increased. They had to make their way back towards the entrance before it got too dark. She did not like the idea of spending the night in the deep forest that they knew very little about, but it was looking like they would have little choice. The forest was growing darker quickly, and the white fog also seemed to grow thicker with every step they took.

Leena followed closely behind Dax as he rushed down the path and back out to where the trees first began to grow dense. She glanced back at Roki, who was still following closely behind them. As she turned her head back towards the front, she came to a sudden halt. Dax was stopped dead in front of her. The thick fog prevented her from seeing what had caused Dax to stop moving. She quickly drew her bow back and crept forward slowly. The sound of heavy boots behind her let her know that Roki had closed in to inspect as well.

She moved forward next to Dax and gasped at the confusing sight in front of her. The path was completely gone. The rugged grass and dirt trail ended abruptly at a thick wall of trees that completely closed in the area, cutting off the direction in which they had come. Leena stood in disbelief.

"How is this possible?" she questioned.

She turned to Dax, who had a serious, concerned look on his face.

"It's the forest," Dax answered, his eyes narrowing.

"I doubt we would be the first adventurers to fall victim to its dark magic," he said.

Leena couldn't help but consider the notion as she thought about all the rumors concerning the forest. Up until that moment, she had just passed the stories off as typical tavern talk. But now, as she stared ahead at the unbelievable scene in front of her, she started to consider the possibility that maybe there was something sinister about the forest. Roki rushed up from behind and stopped at her left side, staring wide-eyed ahead.

"This can't be possible" Roki said, shaking his head in disbelief. "What are we supposed to do now?"

Dax turned around and looked back down the enclosed path in the direction of the deep forest.

"There's only one thing we can do, we must get out of this thick fog so at least we can defend ourselves in the event of an attack. We find a clearing and set up camp until morning," Dax said firmly.

Roki's expression seemed to bounce between agitation and nervousness.

"It's getting nearly too dark to see. We are going to need some light," Roki said as he pulled the unlit torches from his bag.

A few sparks from Dax's sword against a small stone easily set the small torches aflame. Leena tried to keep her eyes peeled and focused as she advanced forward, walking between the dim light from the two torches that Roki and Dax held. But the heavy fog still made it difficult to see. She knew that she wouldn't be able to count on her excellent vision as she normally did. She would instead have to focus intently on her good sense of hearing. Creaks and echoes in the distance all around them made her uneasy.

Occasionally a very distant howl or shriek would cause her to draw back her bow to near full draw, anticipating the worst. She didn't like not being able to see her enemies. She had grown quite comfortable with her special abilities, the most useful of which was her ability to see in complete darkness. Even in complete darkness she could normally still see a faint outline of her surroundings, but the thick fog rendered her nearly blind. The noises grew louder as they echoed all around them. Just then she picked up the very specific sound of a small branch snapping in the distance, a hundred or so feet behind them.

"Something is behind us," she whispered to the others.

Dax shot back a concerned look and stared silently into the dark fog.

"What is it?" Dax whispered.

Leena focused hard and listened. She tried to pick up on the distinct characteristics that would reveal what it was that was following them. She could hear the wind whistling through the branches high above.

She could hear the creeks and moans of the dark forest all around. *SNAP*. There it was again. She couldn't tell what made the noise, but it was getting closer fast.

"We have to move now!" she said, trying not to yell.

Dax spun around with haste and bolted down the path. Leena charged in behind him, trying to stay close so that they wouldn't lose sight of each other. It was difficult to keep her eyes on him as he sprinted ahead at full speed. Every few seconds he disappeared, and she would have to speed up to regain sight of him. Even the dim light from Dax's torch would disappear briefly as the fog would roll around behind him. She struggled to maintain a clear view.

Dax disappeared again suddenly as he quickly veered off to the left. Leena turned the sharp corner behind him and pushed forward. Quickening her pace, she caught a small glimpse of Dax before he disappeared into the white cloud again. A slight rub of Roki's shoulder reassured her that he was still right behind her.

Dax's shape emerged just long enough for her to see him turn sharply again down the curving path. She rounded the corner right behind him and tried to move in close, but it was difficult to keep up. She turned another corner, then another, rushing into the fog after him.

As she moved through another thick patch, she came to an abrupt halt as Dax's crouching shape appeared in front of her. She quickly dropped down as she drew in close.

"This fog is too thick to navigate this trail accurately. I have no idea where I'm going," Dax said, as close to a panic as Leena had ever seen him.

As she tried to think about the situation, Roki appeared suddenly from the thick fog and slid into a crouching position behind them. He looked very uneasy, with large beads of sweat beginning to drip from his forehead.

"Are we still being followed Leena?" Roki asked.

Focusing again on her hearing, she tried to pick up any sounds of movement. She could hear her friends' heavy breathing from all the running they had just done. She could hear their boots grind into the dirt below as their heavy breaths caused small changes in their positions. Even her own controlled breathing was audible, along with the sound of her heart thumping quietly in her chest.

She listened harder for any other sounds, but there was nothing. It was very odd. There didn't seem to be a single sound coming from the forest around them. No wind. No insects chirping. No distance howls or echoes. Nothing. She was quickly becoming very uneasy. Her two friends sat silently, waiting for her response.

"Somethings not right out there, guys," she said in a slightly alarmed tone.

"I can't pick up on a single sound beyond the three of us right here. It's like everything is just gone."

Leena didn't even understand her own words as they finished leaving her tongue. Dax, who never looked shaken, was now starting to develop a severely concerned demeanor.

"Okay, well, we can't stay here. We need to get out of this fog," Dax said, pointing down the path in front of them.

"But stay close together. No telling what kind of danger could be waiting for us this deep in the forest."

Chapter V

With every step they took the forest seemed to grow darker. They forged ahead slowly through the foggy forest until they reached an area where the path forked into multiple directions. "Which way?" Dax whispered behind him. Leena peered through the heavy white cloud at the three identical looking paths in front of her. She listened to see if any of the paths echoed with movement, but she couldn't pick anything up. Finally, she returned an indecisive look.

After a moment of her and Roki failing to decide, Dax nodded towards the path on the right and moved on ahead. The sound of Roki's heavy boots colliding with the dirt let her know he was close behind her. She could barely make out through the fog the shape of the trees that lined the path. They had quickly grown from large and healthy to slender and crooked.

The gnarled trees intertwined tightly with one another, maintaining a thick barrier. She didn't like this part of the forest. There was something odd about it. She felt strange, as if she was being watched. She refocused on the movement in front of her as Dax pulled ahead. A thick cloud of white fog rushed up suddenly, enveloping him completely. She rushed quickly into the fog to close the distance, but she couldn't catch a glimpse of him. He had to have pulled further ahead than she thought.

Her moderate pace quickly turned into a sprint as she worked to close the distance between them. Large clouds of the thick fog rolled left and right, covering any signs of his position. The forest had grown almost completely dark, making it even more difficult to see ahead with the faint glow of Dax's torch illuminating the path.

After running for a good distance with no sign of Dax, she decided to stop and wait for Roki to catch up before continuing. Several moments passed and Roki still hadn't caught up to her. Where was he? She crouched down low to the ground and listened, waiting to hear the sound of Roki's heavy boots colliding with the ground behind her. She couldn't hear anything. Not one single sound. She knew she couldn't yell for them because she didn't know what, or who, else was out there. She also knew she couldn't stay in one spot because it made her an easy target to anything that might be stalking her.

Just as she was about to move forward she heard a sound. It was faint and far ahead, but it sounded familiar. As she focused her hearing, the sound became clearer. It was Dax, he was yelling for help. Whatever had been following them earlier must have found him.

Leena took off running towards Dax's voice, not caring about her inability to see what was ahead. She followed the path as it turned sharply to the right, and then to the left. She passed through several corners as she charged forward, ready to defend her friend from whatever threatened him. After a moment, she came to a part of the path where the thick wall of trees began to recede away, opening up into a larger area. She walked forward cautiously.

Dax's cry for help had faded into silence and her visibility was considerably compromised due to how dark it had become. As she searched ahead, she pulled back hard on her bowstring, bringing the nocked arrow up right beside her head. She looked down the narrow shaft next to her eye, trying to pick out even the slightest of movements. The only images visible were the slight outlines of the dense clouds of fog as they swirled around a few feet in front of her. It was difficult to discern if the movements were from the fog or something else.

She moved ahead as the fog grew more damp, making it much harder to breathe. It seemed to stick to the inside of her lungs. The heavy fog had also adopted a foul, musty smell. It smelled as if it had been sitting in one spot for a hundred years. The stench made her stomach turn.

She pressed ahead aimlessly, hoping to come across her friend at any moment. After a few moments, she started to grow discouraged. How would she ever find him in such a thick fog? He could've been anywhere. Suddenly it came to her. She couldn't believe that she hadn't thought of it before. She had to find her way to the trees and climb high into the branches overhead. That would put her above the fog and maybe just give her a little bit of light to see with.

She turned quickly to her right and walked ahead slowly. After just a moment she caught a faint silhouette of the twisted tree trunks. She stuck the arrow back in her quiver and threw her long wooden bow over her shoulder as she shimmied quickly up the cold smooth tree.

Higher and higher she climbed until the nearly pitch black darkness became just bright enough to see some vague outlines. She looked down at the foggy ground below. It was a large enclosed area, maybe a hundred feet across. The only path leading out was the one she had entered through. It was a dead end. Dax and Roki must have made their way in a different direction. She would have to drop back down and retrace her steps, and fast. No telling what kind of trouble they were in.

She decided to listen for their voices again before heading back the other way. She figured the added altitude would help her pick out the sounds more easily. She listened intently. There was nothing but darkness and silence. Suddenly she heard something. It sounded like Dax calling her name again. But there was something strange about the way it sounded. It had an odd tone to it, an unnatural tone, almost like someone was imitating his voice. The sound sent chills through her entire body. Whoever or whatever was out there, it wasn't Dax. It had led her right where it wanted her to be. She had been careless. She had neglected her own rules and her heightened senses had failed her.

The sound of branch swaying overhead let her know all that she needed to. Whatever it was, it was right above her, and she didn't have time for a plan. It was ready to attack. She only had one option.

A single bead of sweat rolled down the side of her face. With all her strength, she pushed off of the branch she was perched on, sending herself flying into the air, her body easily close to twenty feet above the hard ground below. In one quick motion, she spun around and grabbed her bow from her shoulder. She loaded an arrow and drew back hard on the string, her eyes desperately trying to trace the movements of her invisible stalker.

At the last moment, she caught the dark flash of an outline that gave away the creature's position. It was moving right towards her. She aimed a few inches off center to account for the creature's movement, and released. The arrow exploded off of the string with a vengeance, slicing through the air towards the shadowy outline. Just as the arrow should've connected with its target, a sudden jerk of the shadowy figure sent the arrow deflecting off into the darkness behind it.

Her eyes frantically searched through the mess of shadowy lines in front of her face. She searched for any kind of recognizable shape that would let her know what manner of enemy she was about to face, but everything was moving too fast to focus. She only had a second or two before the force of gravity would finish pulling her down to the ground below. Just then her eye caught a dark shape as its movements flashed in front of her. Whatever it was, it was big, and it was closing in fast. It would be on her in a split second. She didn't have time to plan a strategy. She had time for one move.

With every bit of speed and strength she had, she swung her bow around underneath of the incoming attacker and lifted up hard. She let out a feminine grunt as she heaved the large creature overhead behind her. Just as it cleared her body, something struck her hard in the top of the head, sending her spiraling out of control towards the ground.

The impact happened just a split second sooner than what she had anticipated. Her spinning body came to a sudden stop as it slammed violently into the rock and dirt below, causing her to let out a painful scream. The pain to her ribcage was horrendous, but she knew there was no time to coddle an injury. Now that she was off guard, the creature's next attack was probably imminent. She pushed off of the hard ground with her hands, sending her up into the air and onto her feet. The movement sent pain streaking through her chest and side.

Within half a second she had another arrow nocked and ready to fire. Her ribcage throbbed with pain as she breathed in. Her grip tightened on the smooth leather bow handle as her eyes scanned the area all around her. Being completely immersed in the fog once again, she could hardly see a thing. Every half second or so, a rolling fog would trick her eyes and she would almost release her bowstring before realizing that there was nothing there. She tried to focus her hearing, but she could only hear silence.

She spun around quickly in every direction, waiting for her foe's next attack. Just then her perched ears caught a sound. It was the sound of a small twig snapping off to her left. She crouched down and turned in the direction of the noise, aiming straight ahead into the fog.

Anticipation with a small amount of fear caused her hands to shake ever-so-slightly. She had no idea what was in front of her. She sat crouched, waiting for something to explode through the fog in front of her at any second. Her right ear perked up as the sound of another snapping branch echoed directly behind her. She swung around quickly, ready for the attack. Just as she was sure its attack would come, she heard another branch break, then another. Soon, small sounds were firing off all around her position.

Her heart nearly dropped into her stomach as she realized what was happening. It wasn't just one enemy. It was several enemies, and they were spread out all over. She knew there was little time to react. There was no way she could take on the group with her bow, she wouldn't be able to aim and fire fast enough. She would have to use her blades.

She silently set her bow and arrow onto the ground and without hesitation drew her twin daggers from the sheathing on the sides of her waist. She gripped the handles hard and braced for the attack.

All of the sudden something caught her eye off to the right. The dark mass burst through the swirling clouds of fog with blinding speed, barreling right towards her. She struggled to make out a definite shape, but the advancing creature was moving too fast, almost as if it was weightless. Just as the dark silhouette closed in on her, she dropped backwards and rolled. She could feel the force of the wind rushing by as the creature's attack narrowly missed her body.

She swiftly jumped back to her feet, ready to sink her daggers into her attacker but it had disappeared into the fog again. With no time to think, she heard another snapping noise and rolled around just in time to see the next advance.

The agile creature exploded out of the dense fog slightly off to her left. The dark mass flew through the air effortlessly. She could barely make out several strange looking shapes moving independently of one another. She threw her weight back hard, bending almost completely backwards. She could feel something smooth slide across her arm, followed by a painfully sharp sting as the creature passed over her body. She let out a quiet gasp. She could feel the warm blood run all the way down her arm, but she knew it wasn't severe. It was just a graze.

She leaned back up and dropped into her defensive position. She had no idea how many of the creatures were hunting her, but she did know that she couldn't afford to keep taking hits. She had to land a blow, and fast. She focused her breathing and tried to slow her heart rate. *TH-THUMP, TH-THUMP, TH-THUMP*.

She had never been in a fight where she couldn't rely on her special abilities. When no one else could see, she could see. When no one else could hear, her mind painted vividly every detail of the movement in her surroundings. But this time was different. This time she was blind, deaf, and alone. This time she felt naked in a way she had never known before. All she had were her daggers and a vague outline of movement when something got close to her.

The sound of another branch breaking sent her spinning around in the opposite direction. A second later another cracking sound caught her attention off to the left. Just as she turned her head back towards the direction of the first sound something leaped out of the fog, moving quickly through the air right towards her. She didn't have time to think. She had to strike.

She gripped the dagger hard in her right hand and spun around counterclockwise. Just as the creature reached her, she side-stepped the attack and brought the dagger around, slamming it into the creature's hard body. It let out a loud whistle-like cry as the razor-sharp dagger barely managed to pierce through its tough exterior. She could feel something cold and smooth glide across her arm as it went flying away from her. She listened for the sound of her attacker hitting the ground, but the sound didn't come.

More movement off to her right side caught her attention. She turned to see two or three large shadows darting here and there in front of her. Back off to her left she heard another cracking sound, then another not far from that. Within seconds, branches were moving and snapping all around her. She was surrounded. Her ears instinctively registered each sound and tallied up a rough count. There had to be at least a dozen, probably more. How would she be able to defend herself against so many, especially without being able to see them? She was in trouble.

As the sounds closed in, she knew there was no retreat. There was no getting away. She had to make a stand, no matter what the odds. It would be the battle of her lifetime. She could feel her heart racing in her chest as she glanced around. Three, maybe four, shadows darted in front of her, with more moving all around. They were closing in for the kill. They knew they had her cornered and outnumbered.

One of the creatures off to her right was the first to lunge, and she was ready. As the jolt of movement caught her eye, she turned and hurled her sharp dagger straight at the creature. The impact of the blade into its body caused it to let out a strange noise. She moved quickly aside as the creature sailed past her.

She turned back around as the next creature was already mid-attack. She leaned back and brought her dagger up hard into the creature's body, but the attack was off target, causing the creature to slam into her shoulder, sending her spinning to the ground. She pushed herself up quickly just in time to see the two large shadows hurling towards her.

With no time to react she pushed her feet hard into the ground and jumped up into the air. As the two creatures reached her spinning body, she pushed her legs outwards, landing a hard kick to each of the creatures' bodies. As she spun in the air anticipating her landing, something grabbed onto her left foot and stopped her spin. She slammed hard into the ground with her head and right shoulder taking the brunt of the impact.

The impact caused a violent stream of pain to shoot down her neck and across her shoulders. She rolled over onto her knees, disoriented. She lifted her to scan for the next attack, but it was too late. The pain was nearly unbearable as the sharp objects sank into the soft flesh of her back. She let out an agonizing scream as the fiery pain ran through her back and down her shoulders.

She swung her arm behind her back viciously, sinking the sharp dagger into her attacker's body. She let out another scream as the creature pulled the two sharp objects out of her and retreated backwards. She could feel the warm blood pour out of the two deep wounds on her back. She was badly injured, and she knew it.

She couldn't fight them off. They were too fast. They were too sneaky. She only had one chance. She had to run blindly towards the direction she thought the exit was in and hope for the best. It was her only chance.

Without hesitation she slammed her feet into the ground hard, sending her flying ahead into a full-on sprint. She tucked her head down and ran as fast as she could. She could feel the wind rush past her as the stalking creatures lunged at her and missed. She ran forward at incredible speed, not stopping to look behind. She could hear the rustling noises as the creatures charged after her. She couldn't see anything but darkness ahead. It was pitch black. She took quick deep breaths as she sped forward.

Just then, Leena slammed into something hard. It didn't hurt, but it stopped her dead in her tracks. It felt like a mess of tangled vines. She tried to push forward but it was strong. It pulled back at her. It moved slightly as she pushed but it was too tough. She couldn't get through. She had to turn around before the creatures reached her. As she went to turn her head, fear struck her. She was stuck. The net-like structure was grabbing onto her, holding her still. She tried hard to move but it was useless. The strands were stuck to her like they were covered in sticky sap. She was completely immobilized.

She struggled hard to free herself from the sticky mess, but it was no use. The harder she struggled the more tired she became. She felt strange. Her body was weak, and her mind was swimmy. The silhouettes in front of her danced and split into twos and threes. It wasn't a natural feeling. What was going on?

Her arms went limp as she lost control of her muscles, her head dropping to the side. Her body hung motionless, attached firmly to the sticky net. Her mind was disoriented but she could still think just clearly enough to put the pieces together. She must've been poisoned when the creature stabbed her in the back.

What kind of poisonous creature had agility like that, she wondered? Horror struck her as she realized that what she was now stuck onto wasn't a net at all. It was a web. She had wandered into a nest, filled with vile, prey-mimicking spiders. She was the prey and her hunters would reach her at any second.

As her nearly lifeless body hung there she was filled with an indescribable sense of regret. Many questions ran through her mind. How had the wretched creatures been able to mimic her friend's voice? Had they somehow read her mind? Had they heard him call for her, or had her friends shared the same fate as she was about to? Fear tore at her mind. She forced one last breath as her tired heart slowed to a crawl and her disoriented mind faded until it was a quiet black nothingness. She was gone.

Chapter VI

TH-THUMP, TH-THUMP, TH-THUMP. The dull movement throbbed in Leena's chest as her heart struggled to push blood through her limp body. With some effort she managed to force her heavy eyelids open slightly. It was still dark all around her. She tried to focus her squinted eyes, but it was no use. Her vision was compromised between the dizziness and complete darkness.

She relaxed her straining eye muscles and let her eyelids drop quickly back down. Relaxing felt good. Her body was aching and sore. Her muscles didn't want to move. She tried to move her arms, but they wouldn't budge. They were held tightly against her body. They felt numb. Her legs were the same way, held tightly together.

As she awakened a little bit more she realized that her whole body was bound together. She was completely immobilized. It was even hard to breathe.

It was so tight she couldn't even move her body from side to side. Then she remembered about the creatures that were hunting her previously, before she had fainted. They could've been anywhere. They probably wrapped her up in the webbing to save her for a snack.

Several different versions of her imminent fate flashed in her mind, none of which she was very fond of. She had to do something, but what could she do? She was completely unable to move. The muscles in her throat hadn't awakened enough yet to scream for help. Not to mention, screaming would draw attention to her, if she wasn't the center of attention already. Fear poured into her mind as she thought about her predicament.

Suddenly, something caught her attention. It was a smell. It was foul and musty, like rotting meat in an abandoned cottage. It smelled damp, old. The heavy scent rested on her lungs like a blanket, making every shallow, painful breath much less appealing. She struggled to force one of her sleeping limbs into movement, but the venom still had a strong effect on her body. Even if she managed to get free from her bindings, she knew that she wouldn't be able to walk.

Her attention returned to her surroundings as she picked up an odd noise. It was an almost mechanical-like clicking noise coming from a few feet in front of her. She listened intently. The sound grew louder and louder, until it was right in front of her face. She felt a rush of warm, moist air glide across her face, followed by the same foul smell. But this time the smell was much stronger. The musty air was saturated with it. It made it almost impossible to breathe. Every time she would inhale, her body would choke on the rancid air and force her lungs to push it back out.

More clicking noises followed behind the first and moved closer to her. Her heart nearly stopped as she felt something brush down the right side of her face. It was smooth and cold. Next it started at her shoulder and moved all the way down to her thigh. Her heart started to pound harder, causing a broad pain across her chest.

Her weakened heart muscle struggled to send adrenaline flowing through her veins in anticipation of what came next. Fear gripped her as she realized how helpless she was. She couldn't move. She couldn't breathe. She didn't have a chance. What could she do? A sea of regret and anger flooded her mind. How could she have been so careless? How could she have let the creatures out smart and out maneuver her? It should've been her stalking them. But none of that mattered now. It was too late. She had made a mistake, and it would cost her everything.

The clicking noises closed in all around her. She could feel the area sway back and forth as the creatures surrounded her position. Her eyes squeezed themselves shut as she braced for what she knew was coming. The creatures were ready for their meal, and she was it. There was no way out. Her weak heart throbbed in her chest. Any moment one of the creatures would sink their sharp teeth into her limp body and feed off her blood. She knew how it worked, how agonizing it would be. She had never been so scared in her life.

She could feel the musty air swirl around in front of her face as the creature reared back to attack. Out of pure reflex she tightened every sleepy muscle in her body, anticipating the bite. The large web swayed again as the creature shot its rearing body back down towards her, its deadly fangs slicing through the air towards her jugular. She braced herself for the bite.

All at once, a blinding flash of light tore through the area. Even behind her closed eyes the light sent a streaking pain through her head. Her attackers were just as surprised by it as she was. She could feel the area jolt and sway as the startled creatures scattered quickly outward. The source of the brilliant yellow-orange light moved and darted around a good distance in front of her. Her excellent hearing was starting to return to her. She could pick out the sounds of boots smacking the dirt. It was human. *They*, were human. There were two of them.

"LEENA?" the male voice called.

Her heart fluttered as she recognized the familiar voice. She struggled to force out a cry, but the effects of the venom had not completely worn off. All that came out was a pathetic squeal. With a forced effort she peeled her eyelids open, flooding her vision with blinding yellow light. Her head pounded. Holding her eyes open was agonizing. Her vision danced and weaved as it struggled to adjust from complete darkness to bright light.

After a moment the two or three undiscernible scenes converged into one fuzzy picture. She could see two figures in front of her quite a distance away. Each held a brightly lit torch in their hands. It was hard to make out any details through her hazy vision, but she would know those two figures anywhere. It was Dax and Roki. Her friends were alive.

A strong feeling of relief filled her heavy heart. She looked on as the torches grew closer and illuminated a good portion of the area. Even the lingering fog could not shield the light of the torches. Through her compromised view she could see the damp enclosure surrounding the area. There were large rocks around the outsides, with dark holes burrowed into the ground. Large, grey webs covered some of the holes. More webbing shot from rock to rock. She felt more jerking and jolting as the creatures lunged from the area, heading towards her friends.

As the light from the torches made the creatures visible for the first time, their vile figures filled her with horror. Chills ran down her spine as she watched the way the nearly five-foot-tall spiders stalked their prey. Their eight slender legs scattered gracefully across the ground around them as they darted back and forth through the shadows. The spiders were shiny black, with grey streaks running down their backs and long sharp fangs perched on the fronts of their mouths.

She could feel the tired muscles in her neck strain as she looked down at her body. It was completely immobilized by a tight wrapping of sticky white spider-web. She leaned her tired head over to the side and looked around. Her body wrap was stuck onto a much larger web that stretched from the ground beneath her, up into the black darkness above.

"LEENA?" the familiar voice echoed again.

It felt so good to hear Dax's voice. She squirmed slightly and tried to call out. Her voice was a little more audible than before, but not by much. As she looked down in front of her, she quickly realized that Dax and Roki were not aware of the creatures that stalked them. They were too busy searching for her. She had to warn them. With every ounce of strength, she pulled in a deep breath. She squeezed the muscles of her throat and lungs all at once and cried out loudly.

"Look Out!" She yelled.

She could see Dax's head jolt towards her direction. He had heard her. They seemed to heed her warning as they tossed the flaming torches off into the brush beside them. Within a second or two the torches ignited the small shrubs, sending large flames into the air. As the orange flames brightened the dark shadows, Dax and Roki quickly spotted the group of crafty spiders. There was nothing she could do but watch the scene unfold.

Dax drew his sword up high, with his shield readied out in front. Roki reached back with his large arms and drew out his heavy hammer. Her two friends walked back slowly as the spiders moved in to surround them. There was easily a dozen of the wretched creatures. Her disoriented ears could just barely pick up Roki's muffled voice.

"Spiders," Roki growled, "It had to be spiders."

All at once the battle began. It was hard to focus on the movement, but she could see the creatures darting here and there, along with weapons swinging. She caught a glimpse of a spider landing on Dax's back just as Roki's heavy hammer slammed into its side, sending bright green blood spraying across the ground. Her eyes throbbed. More shadows and light rays flashed in front of her.

Her vision focused on Dax as he spun around hard and swung his sharp sword through the air perfectly, slicing one of the spiders' bodies open wide. He stepped to the side as the green blood and insides exploded outwards. Roki landed another hit as his massive hammer came crushing down on top of a spider, causing it to make a quick, sharp noise as its body was crushed against the hard ground. Another spider lunged at Roki before he could maneuver his hammer.

"Down!" Dax shouted.

Roki dropped and leaned to his right as Dax jumped forward and thrust his sword straight into the belly of the attacking spider. With one smooth motion he pulled the blade out and went into a spinning sidestep as the shrieking creature went flying past him. As the spider landed, its black body began to convulse heavily as bright green blood poured out onto the ground.

Roki and Dax spun around to face the rest of the spiders. Roki's hammer caught the next spider mid-air, sending its mangled body flying into the burning brush pile. A flash of flame was followed by a shrill shriek. Dax ducked down and rolled as the next spider attacked. As it sailed overhead, Dax stopped mid-roll and thrust hard upwards, slicing the back legs of the spider clean off. Roki brought his hammer around to finish it off. The hammer collided with its body, followed by a satisfying crunching sound as the green liquid sprayed upwards into the air. Dax and Roki recovered quickly and turned towards the remaining spiders.

Only a small handful of the spiders now stood in front of them, hissing and shifting back and forth. Leena tried to focus her eyes as she waited for the last attacks. Several seconds passed by and the creatures still hadn't moved. They just hissed and shifted around back and forth. Finally, Roki gripped his hammer and charged forward. Dax was right next to him, sword readied. As they got close, the spiders jerked in reflex, jumping backwards several feet. Dax and Roki came to a halt as the scared creatures darted off into the trees and disappeared.

They stood staring into the dark overgrown trees for a few moments until they finally realized the spiders weren't coming back for them. Then they focused their attention on finding Leena.

"Leena!" Dax called out loudly. Roki also began calling out for her.

"Leena!" they shouted together.

She could feel some of the strength starting to return to her muscles. She focused her breath hard and cried out loudly.

"Over here! In the trees!" she cried with a hoarse squeal.

The two adventurers turned to her voice and began running towards her. She looked down as Dax and Roki stood at the foot of the large, sticky spider-web, looking up at her wrapped body.

"Leena!" Roki said in an excited voice as he realized she was okay.

"Help me cut her down, Roki," Dax said quickly.

Leena watched as Dax and Roki rubbed their hands over an unlit torch, coating them thoroughly in the thick oil. Once they had oiled up their hands and the bottom of their boots, they reached up and grabbed onto the thin, sticky web. She could feel the whole web sway as they climbed.

When her two friends reached her, they stopped and looked at her. She could see the look of relief in their eyes. She could also see that they held themselves responsible for her almost getting killed. She knew it was no one's fault but her own. She hadn't had much experience not being able to use her senses, and because of that, she had been careless, and it almost got her killed. If it hadn't been for her two friends, she wouldn't be alive.

After a few minutes of sawing on the tough strands of web, they finally managed to cut her bindings loose. Roki held onto the last strand of web that was attached to the wrapping and slowly lowered her to the ground as Dax waited beneath to catch her.

Leena sank deep into his arms as Dax grabbed her tightly. He lowered her to the ground slowly and pulled out a small dagger. Roki's heavy boots dropped down onto the ground next to her as Dax sliced through the heavy spider-web wrapped around her body. As the last few strands snapped she could feel the release of pressure. It sent pain radiating all through her back, chest, and shoulders. She gasped for a deep breath. As the air filled her lungs more pain shot through her chest, sending her into a coughing fit. After a few moments her body smoothed out.

"Are you okay?" Dax asked, his face full of worry.

She looked up him through an involuntary flow of tears and forced a smile.

"I'm okay. Thanks to you two."

"I'm sorry I didn't watch out for you better, I should've…"

Leena interrupted Dax's apology.

"It wasn't your fault Dax. It wasn't anyone's fault but my own. I shouldn't have underestimated my surroundings. Besides, it was almost as if the forest was trying to separate us," she said, shuttering at the thought.

Dax seemed to understand as he began to glance around the area. Roki leaned in and put his hand on her shoulder in a friendly embrace.

"I'm just glad you're okay, Leena," Roki said.

She could see him fighting back emotion as she gripped his hand tight and tried to stand up. Her muscles were weak, but she managed to stand onto her feet. Her body swayed back and forth.

"The venom from the spider has affected my body, I'm afraid I won't be of much use in battle for a while," she said.

"Hopefully you won't need to be" Dax replied as he handed her the two small daggers she had dropped when she went unconscious.

She took the daggers with her left hand and struggled to slip them into her belt.

"I spotted your bow on the ground near the entrance. We can grab it on the way out," Roki added.

It was still foggy all around them but the brightness from the flames gave them enough light to spot the path leading out of the spiders' den. Leena limped along as her friends held her up on either side. She could see the mangled spider carcasses littering the hard ground. Shallow pools of bright green liquid settled beneath each body. She was relieved to see the defeated horde. The path leading out was only twenty or so feet away and she felt more relieved with every step. She was more than ready to get as far away from the dark and vile den as possible, so she could forget all about it. It was her first experience with defeat, and she vowed to herself that it would be her last.

Chapter VII

The exit was only a few feet away. Leena fought to force her nearly limp legs to cooperate. With a great effort she awkwardly placed one foot in front of the other and leaned on her two friends for support as they made their way toward the exit. The path leading out of the spiders' den was in close view. They were nearly out.

Suddenly something caught her attention. A loud cracking noise thundered overhead. She came to a halt and peered up into the darkness above them. It was too dark to see anything. Another loud noise sounded off. Leena glanced nervously at her friends as they stared up into the black shadow above, their alerted expressions revealing their deep concern.

As she listened for audible clues that might reveal the cause of the commotion, she immediately picked up on a strange noise. It was a faint shaking noise, shimmying. It wasn't an unfamiliar sound, yet the odd repetition made her uneasy. She glanced over at a nearby tree branch and watched as the small limbs swayed slightly from side to side, causing the leaves the rustle. Something was moving through the tree tops. Leena looked back at her friends and nodded her head towards the rustling leaves. The two of them stared silently at the moving tree limbs for a moment, studying them, before a look of deep concern formed on Dax's face. His eyes narrowed.

"We need to move, now," Dax said.

She could feel Roki's big arm lift her body in response to Dax's order. She held on tight as they rushed forward, her feet scarcely touching the ground. The exit was only a dozen or so feet. They would be out of the den in just a moment.

They came to an abrupt halt as the branches above the exit jolted violently. Leena's eyes instinctively scanned the swaying tree limbs, looking for the source of the movement. The thick fog had risen into the tree tops making it hard to see, even with the dimly burning brush behind them.

There was a quick flash of movement above, followed by another violent swaying of the tree branches. Something was moving towards them, and whatever it was, it was big. She had to warn them of the danger. Just as she was about to let out the warning, she was interrupted by a deafening crash as something slammed onto the ground in front of them.

The heavy impact caused the ground to shake beneath her feet and she struggled to keep her balance. As the movement settled, her heart sank. Something very large now blocked the only exit.

Leena looked up at the fifteen-foot-tall creature, terrified. It had the same shape and characteristics of the creatures that had nearly ended her life only minutes ago. She knew exactly what it was, but she didn't want to accept it. It was a spider. Its giant body was covered with smooth black skin. It had empty black eyes covering its head and long sharp fangs protruding out of its mouth. The spider queen was looking for her babies, and she wasn't happy.

The giant creature reared back and let out a deafening shriek. The sound was painful. Leena dropped to her knees with her hands covering her ears in an effort to muffle the shrill ringing. Dax and Roki still stood next to her, their hands cupped in a similar manner. Without further warning, the giant spider lunged towards them with surprising speed. One of its massive front legs collided with Dax's body before he could manage to raise his shield, sending him flying backwards. Roki took advantage of the opportunity and drew up his heavy hammer. He put all his force into a mighty swing but before it could connect, another flash of a giant black spider leg sent him flying off in the opposite direction.

The massive creature was only a foot or two in front of her now, approaching fast. She was helpless. Her body hadn't recovered enough from the venom to be of any help in the fight. The spider stopped in front of her and let out another loud squeal. Her head throbbed with pain as the noise rang out. She dropped her head and clenched her ears in agony. Her head felt as if it could explode from the pressure and pain.

Dax's form caught her eye as he charged back in towards the creature. He lunged forward and jabbed his sword hard into the creature, but the thick shiny covering was like armor. Dax's sword only penetrated an inch or two, causing the giant spider to let out an aggravated sounding snarl. It jolted around towards Dax and swung one of its front legs at him.

The large black leg collided with Dax's knees, sending him spinning in the air before landing hard on the ground. He looked up just in time to see the sharp-edged spider leg barreling down towards his body. He managed to bring his shield up just in time to block the attack. The sharp spear-like leg slammed into his shield, pushing it down into his chest. Dax let out a painful screech.

The spider quickly drew back its leg again for a second attack, but before it could attack again, Roki caught it off-guard with a hard strike of his hammer. The heavy steel collided with the creature's back legs sending it spinning off balance. Dax wasted no time as he rolled onto his feet and jumped at the creature.

He shoved his sword hard into the spider's armor-like body. Again, it only penetrated three or four inches. The giant spider let out another furious snarl and slammed its front legs into Dax's chest. His body looked like a ragdoll as it went spinning into the air. Leena's heart dropped as she saw Dax fly off into the brush. She turned her attention back to Roki who was just landing his next attack.

The massive swing sent the heavy hammer slamming into the creature's left side. The impact caused the spider's thick shiny body to let out a cracking noise as it slid a few feet backwards. Despite the strong impact, the attack didn't seem to faze it. The creature quickly rolled back onto its feet and lunged towards Roki. It swung up its front legs into Roki's body, sending him flying high up into the trees. She could hear branches breaking as Roki crashed into the tree branches above.

The creature turned again towards her, drool pouring from its open mouth. She could see a few beads of green liquid running down the side of its body. Dax's sword attacks were barely a flesh wound. It focused its view on her once again and charged. She drew one of the daggers from her waist and hurled it towards the creature, but her muscles were still weak. The small dagger wobbled through the air, sailing right past the creature. The small blade struck a tree behind and dropped to the ground with a clanking noise.

The giant spider closed the remaining distance quickly and reared back to attack. Leena braced for the attack. Just then Dax appeared from the high brush to the left and rolled in front of her. He brought his sword up hard with every ounce of strength he had.

The force of the spider's attack, coupled with all of Dax's strength, drove the sword deep into the creature's belly. Green liquid sprayed out onto the ground as the spider let out a loud shriek. It reared back again and brought its right front leg down hard. The sharp shiny tip tore through Dax's shoulder with ease, pinning him down on top of her.

Dax's painful scream rang inside of her ears, sending pain shooting across the back of her head. She looked up just in time to see Roki's large shape lunge out of the high tree tops above. His large frame and heavy hammer caused him to drop fast, sending him barreling down towards the ground below. Just as he reached the creature, he brought down his hammer with a mighty force, slamming it into the spider's head. The hammer collided with a loud noise as green gooey liquid sprayed outwards.

Before Roki could land on the ground, the spider's other front leg slammed into his body. It tore through his side easily, causing him to release a blood-curdling scream. His large body slammed into the ground a couple feet to Leena's right side. He wasn't moving. It didn't look good. The creature flexed its right leg, causing the sharp tip to twist inside of Dax's shoulder. He screamed in agony. She had to do something, or it was over for them. But what could she do?

She glanced over at Roki who was pinned down to the ground. He writhed in pain, virtually unable to move. As the dim light from burning leaves in the background sent shadows dancing across the ground, suddenly something caught her eye next to Roki's head. It was her bow. It had fallen to the ground earlier and it still had an arrow ready to fire. She stretched to reach for it but Dax's body was pressed down hard on top of hers, preventing her from reaching farther. It was just out of reach by a finger's length.

She struggled to wiggle her body free. With every movement Dax grunted with pain. Her fingers could almost touch it. The giant spider reared back its ugly black head again, this time for the kill. Its long sharp fangs dripped with venom as it locked its gaze on Dax. It let out a shriek and lurched forward. Leena reached up, stretching every muscle fiber in her right arm. As her fingers touched the smooth wooden bow handle she popped it up into the air with a flicking motion.

Her left hand snatched the bow out of the air as she grabbed the arrow with her right to force it back onto the rest. In one fluid motion she set the arrow and slid her hand down onto the string, pulling back hard with every ounce of strength she still had. She could feel her weak arm muscles shaking as she struggled to pull the bowstring back to full draw. It was her only chance. The shot had to be perfect.

She waited until the spider's head was almost to Dax's body before she focused her aim and released. The back of the arrow kicked out to the side as it exploded off of the bow string with surprising force. It flexed and swayed violently as it tore through the air towards the vile creature. Just as the spider's long fangs nearly reached their mark, the wobbly arrow collided with the spider's head.

Even with dim lighting and a bad release, she had managed to nail her target almost perfectly. The arrow sliced through one of the spider's dark beady eyes and exploded out of the back of its head where Roki's hammer strike had weakened it. The spider let out an unbearable high-pitched squeal and thrashed violently around. The sharp pointed legs ripped out from Dax and Roki's bodies causing them to scream out in pain. Leena covered her ears once again to dull the pain from the loud noise. She watched as the creature thrashed and convulsed backwards until finally rolling onto its back.

After a few seconds of the creature being motionless and silent, she realized it was dead. Its long shiny legs were now curled up close to its body, making it look much smaller than it had before. As she was looking at the dead giant spider, suddenly brilliant blue flames engulfed its shiny black carcass. The bright blue fire burned hot and fast. It quickly disintegrated the carcass into ash and within a few seconds it was gone.

Almost immediately, the forest around them started to change. The dark shadows seemed to get lighter and the fog thinned out and started to fall to the ground like clear mist before their eyes. Her ears picked up the sound of the wind and the other normal forest sounds returning. It was like the spiders had some kind of dark effect on the forest. Leena dropped her head to the ground and exhaled a deep, tired, sigh of relief.

Looking up, it seemed as though the forest ceiling had parted, revealing a small patch of evening sky overhead. She looked over at Dax who was now on his feet, gripping his wounded shoulder, staring back at her. It was easy to see that he was in pain but he seemed equally relieved that the dark creatures were gone. Leena's attention then shifted to Roki, who was lying nearly unconscious on the ground next to her. His wound didn't look bad enough to be fatal, but the fall had probably hurt him quite a bit. He would need a lot of rest.

She could feel her strength starting to return in a small degree as she stood slowly to her feet. She swung her bow onto her back and limped over to where her dagger had fallen. It was easy to spot against the hard ground. She grabbed the dagger and slipped it back into her belt. Then she limped back over to where Roki was laying. Dax had sheathed his sword and shield and was already next to him, kneeling on the ground.

"Are you okay, Roki?" Dax asked in a concerned voice as he looked over his wound. Roki peeled open his tired looking eyes and looked up at Dax.

"I think I'll live," Roki answered in a rough voice. "You may need to help me to my feet though."

Leena grabbed onto one arm as Dax grabbed the other and they both lifted him to his feet. Roki clenched his teeth in pain as the injured muscles in his midsection were forced to support his weight. Dax grabbed Roki's hammer and carried it in his left hand. Slowly they made their way towards the path leading out of the spider's den. Leena shot one last glance back at the musty den and accepted the realization that they were barely walking away with their lives.

Once outside of the spiders' den, she was instantly surprised. The whole manner of the forest seemed different. The fog was now a thin clear mist as it floated only an inch or two off of the ground. The dark forest ceiling had peeled back, revealing the beautiful night sky above. Bright white light from the moon and stars showered the forest floor with a soft white glow, illuminating once again the enticing peacefulness of the forest they had come to know. The twisted dark maze of tree trunks had somehow seemed to thin out into a large clearing with only a few innocent looking paths leading out.

The area was the complete opposite of what it had been before the spider encounter. It was almost as if slaying the giant spider queen had somehow released that part of the forest from its dark bondage. She held onto Roki as they walked him over into the large clearing.

"It seems calm for now," Dax started. "We should set up camp here for tonight. We are all going to need some rest."

Leena looked around at the tranquil scenery for a few seconds before they both lowered Roki onto a soft patch of short green grass. Roki scooted his back up against a large log and immediately closed his eyes. Dax moved away and began making a fire at the center of the grassy area.

Leena bent down and peeled back the blood-soaked garment covering Roki's wound. Warm red blood instantly ran down her hand and onto the ground. It was easy to tell from his facial expression that he was in considerable pain, though his extreme fatigue was helping to mask his agony. Large beads of sweat rolled down his forehead as he grunted through each shallow breath.

After a few seconds of riffling through her belt pouch, she drew out a sharp steel fishing hook. It was much larger than she would've liked, but it would have to do. She had to stop the bleeding. Healing herbs would be ideal but they had used all they had. She would have to resort to more barbaric forms of healing.

"Roki..." she started.

Roki peeled his eyes open with a grunt.

"I'm going to have to stitch up your wound now. It's a large piece of steel and it's going to hurt, a lot," she said.

At her words Roki reached down clumsily at his side and drew up a small wineskin. He reached over with another grunt, peeling back the covering from the top. After a few chugs of the strong wine he replaced the cover and dropped it to his side.

"Okay," he said tiredly, "Just give me a few minutes."

Leena gave him an understanding nod and placed the steel hook back in her pouch. Suturing the wound would be much easier after the wine started to take effect. She looked silently over at Dax, who already had a decent campfire going. He sat close to the yellow flames, on top of a small brown stump. She moved in a little closer to the fire and watched as he removed his leather vest and blood-stained tunic. He pulled the tunic over his head with a groan, his right arm doing most of the work. The wound on his shoulder was small compared to Roki's, but it still looked very painful. Luckily, it wasn't anywhere near fatal. She knew that his superior athleticism would allow him to recover quickly, but still, she felt the need to show concern.

"Are you okay?" she questioned.

Dax looked over at her with a slight smile.

"I'll be okay. It's only a small wound," he answered. "What about you?"

Leena hadn't thought about herself since the spider's den. Somewhere in all the action she had managed to forget about her own injury. Throbbing pain shot down her back as she recollected the spider fangs sinking deep into her flesh. Now that her attention had returned to the injury, it seemed to be much more annoying. The flesh around the two large puncture wounds started to sting and itch. She forced her mind off of it long enough to finish her conversation.

"I will be fine," she answered.

Dax returned an unconvinced stare. "Let me see," he insisted softly.

She stood staring at Dax for a moment, undecidedly, before she finally began unstrapping her green leather armor. Once it was unstrapped, she began removing it piece by piece.

"Don't get any ideas" she said, jokingly. Dax scrunched his eyebrows, as if he didn't know whether she was being serious or making a joke.

"I wouldn't think of it" he returned with an awkward laugh.

Leena finished dropping the rest of her leather covering and then turned around facing away from Dax, with Roki off behind her to the side. With a little hesitation she lifted up on her outer clothing and pulled it over her head, leaving nothing to cover her upper body but a thin, scant under garment. As her dark colored over shirt passed in front of her eyes, she could see the wet blood stains on the back from where she had been bitten. Dropping the garment to the ground, she stood there waiting for Dax's analysis. She could hear his footsteps approach from behind and stop.

Pain shot through her back as his hand touch her skin near the wounds. The injury felt as if it was on fire, but yet his cold hands felt pleasant. They were hard and calloused but also gentle and caring. She could feel the caution in his inspection. She could tell he didn't want to hurt her but at the same time it seemed that he enjoyed touching her skin. She enjoyed it. They had been adventuring together for years but she couldn't remember a time when she and Dax had gotten so close to each other.

It was always the three of them, together, battling dangerous creatures and exploring hidden areas. She had never viewed either of them as anything other than a friend. But now, as Dax glided his gentle hands across her back, she found herself with questions she had never thought about before.

She wondered if the deep friendship she had with Dax could maybe be something more. What would happen between the three of them if she and Dax started to develop feelings for each other? Would pursuing such feelings be worth the cost? She didn't know. All she did know was that everything inside of her wanted him to keep touching her. His touch ignited a feeling in her she had never felt before, something she didn't know if she could control. Maybe she didn't want to control it.

Her body trembled with nervousness and anticipation as the thoughts flashed through her mind. Her heart fluttered as Dax's hands slid across her soft skin and came to rest on her shoulders. His embrace seemed to flood her body with desire. She turned around slowly, her body shaking nervously. As she came around, Dax's eyes met hers with a passionate gaze. She could tell by the way he looked at her that he was feeling a similar notion. His large, dark-colored eyes traveled down her scantily clad body and back up again. The expression on his face let her know that he was trying to restrain himself as hard as she was. It seemed as if he was experiencing the strong feelings for the first time, just as she was. It was new for them both.

She watched his moonlit eyes, patiently but nervously waiting for him to make the next move. She could feel her own eyes begging him to move in closer. Dax slowly leaned in towards her, his mouth moving towards her own. Her heart fluttered again as he closed the distance. Suddenly, a loud noise snapped her out of her daze. Roki was leaning against the log, virtually unconscious, in the middle of a coughing fit.

The noise brought her attention back to the situation she was in. All at once the awkwardness of being nearly naked in front of her long-time friend returned. She glanced back up at Dax who now also appeared to be feeling equally as awkward. He took a nervous step backwards and diverted the attention.

"Your wounds are deep, but I think they will heal up fine," Dax stuttered quickly. Then, reaching down, he grabbed her outer clothing and handed it to her before starting back towards his former position near the fire. Leena stared down at the blood stained dark colored garment, confused by what had just happened. As fast as the carnal emotions had appeared, they were gone, leaving her with only a notion of romantic yearning.

She quickly turned around and slipped her outer garment back over her head. It was a sharp sting as the cloth rubbed against her wounds. Then she picked up her leather armor and strapped each piece back on. Her attention then turned back to Roki, who was plenty relaxed enough for her to work. She walked over to him and knelt to the ground, drawing out one of her sharp daggers.

The sharp steel blade sliced through the soft, blood-stained tunic with ease, revealing his whole midsection. The wound was much larger than she had originally thought. Bright red blood still flowed out slowly from the wound, running down his body and into a small red puddle that had formed on the ground beneath him.

Leena pulled the hook back out of her pouch and tore a few long threads from the piece of Roki's torn tunic. The threads were thicker than she wanted but at least they would be able to close the wound. After waiting a moment to make sure he wasn't going to have another coughing fit, she began the work of stitching him up.

A quick push of the thick metal hook through Roki's bloodied flesh started the thread. His teeth clenched down hard as the metal pierced through. Then she took and poured some of the wine onto the wound to clean it. At this, Roki let out a loud scream and thrashed around. Dax quickly ran over to help hold him still. Dax's eyes met hers with an affectionate gaze and then quickly looked down at Roki's wound. She smiled.

"Are you ready?" she asked.

"Don't worry, I got him," Dax answered.

After the burning from the wine settled down, Roki didn't seem as affected by the hook piercing his flesh. Stitch after stitch she sowed until she tied off the last one. She cut the thread loose from the stitch and placed the items back in her pouch. Roki lay still, fully unconscious, breathing heavily. His large chest moved high and then dropped quickly down. His clothes were drenched in sweat from the pain.

She looked over at Dax, who was still kneeling on the other side of Roki. He stared back at her, though not the way he always had before. The awkwardness from a moment ago seemed to now be gone but she could tell something was different between them. She could tell there was something more.

"We should get some sleep. I'll take first watch" she said, divertingly.

Dax nodded and plopped down in the grass next to Roki. He leaned back against the large log and drew his shiny sword, laying it across his legs. As Dax leaned his head back and closed his eyes, Leena got up and walked over towards the fire. She sat down on top of a large rock a foot or two away.

The warmness from the camp fire soothed her achy body. She closed her eyes and took a deep breath of the misty forest air. It smelled of various kinds of trees and plants. She loved the way the forest smelled at night. It always relaxed her. After a few moments she pulled out a few small pieces of food from her pouch and washed it down with a gulp from the small water bag at her side. She looked over at her two battered friends and then back at the forest. It had been one hell of a day.

As she studied the calm scenery, her mind drifted into thought. The day's events were still very fresh in her mind. A quick pain ran down her shoulder blades as she thought back over the last battle. Shadowy images of the ugly creatures flashed through her mind. She knew the spider's den would haunt her dreams for many nights to come.

Chapter VIII

His surroundings were vague. The light and darkness seemed to intertwine into wavy odd-shaped pillars all around him. Dax tried to focus on the images in front of him, but they drifted and changed before his eyes. Purple and blue clouds of smoke danced and swirled all around, making his mind feel off-balanced.

He focused hard to see what the strange figure in front of him would turn out to be. The mysterious movements seemed to beckon his attention. A ball of golden light formed suddenly in front of his face, hiding behind dark shades of purple shadows. He could hear a faint hum all around him, drawing him in. He could feel the warmth from the light radiating through the cold darkness. His eyes were mesmerized by the brilliant golden sphere as it swirled around.

Dax concentrated on the movements with intrigue as they started to take shape. He looked on in awe as the familiar shape of a woman's face formed in front of him. Her eyes stared into his, begging his attention. Her mouth opened slowly as if she was going to speak. He tried to focus on the sound of her words but there was only silence. She looked as if she desperately wanted to tell him something. The anxiety weighed on his mind as he tried to hear her silent words. What was she saying? Just then a powerful but feminine voice echoed all around him. "Get up, Dax!" the voice thundered.

Dax's heart began to race. *TH-THUMP. TH-THUMP.* The shape of the woman distorted and disappeared as the dark purple shadows rushed in to surround it once more. Violent clashes of light and dark flashed in front of him. His heart beat even faster. "Wake up now!" the voice thundered loudly. The voice was so loud it shook Dax's body.

He opened his eyes and sat up, his heart pounding. He looked all around in a panic. His breathing began to slow as he quickly realized it was only a dream. They were still in the dark forest, with the campfire burning and stars glowing overhead. He took a few deep breaths and let his heart rate return to normal. He looked over at Leena who was sitting next to the fire, now watching him with a concerned look on her face.

"You okay?" Leena questioned. "You were thrashing around quite a bit there."

Dax took another slow deep breath.

"I'm fine. I just had a strange dream is all," he replied.

At his words, Leena went back to staring at the orange flame. After relaxing for a few moments Dax rose to his feet and slipped his sword back into the sheath on his back. The pain from his wounded shoulder had intensified, streaking through his chest as he reached up. He let out a reluctant groan. Some movement to his right side quickly caught his attention. Roki was just gaining consciousness. As soon as Roki's eyes opened, he went into a violent coughing fit. Dax could tell it caused him severe pain with each cough as the muscles in his abdomen were forced to tighten. On the last cough, Dax watched as fresh red blood oozed out of Roki's sutured wound. Roki let out a painful-sounding growl.

"Easy..." Leena said softly as she rushed over to Roki's side. "Here drink some of this."

Dax watched as he kicked the wineskin back and chugged. After a few seconds Roki dropped the wineskin to his side again and relaxed. The wine would dull his body's need to cough, at least for a little while.

"I guess this is what I get for getting sloppy, huh?" Roki said.

"We were all sloppy Roki, just try to relax," Dax said.

Roki made a tired shoulder movement indicating that he somewhat agreed with him and then leaned his head back against the log, staring up at the sky.

Dax looked out into the dark forest around them. They were in the center of a large, grassy clearing. The path leading into the spiders' den was directly behind him, with two paths in front of him that split into a 'V' shape. To the left and right was nothing but thick forest and brush.

He looked at the dark forest to his left and then to his right. It seemed very peaceful and quiet, though it was too dark to see into. As he was about to turn back towards the others something caught his eye. It was a tiny glowing light, no bigger than a bronze coin. It floated about eye-level just inside the tree line. It drifted back and forth behind a narrow tree limb, almost as if it was watching him.

Dax stared at it some more. It was an odd sight, yet something seemed familiar about it. It started to streak around behind the trees as if to catch his attention. He glanced over at his two friends, who seemed to both be lost in their own worlds, and then back at the glowing yellow light. It danced and swayed and moved in and out of the tree branches.

Dax took a few steps forward, trying to get a closer look, but as he moved forward the glowing light drifted back deeper into the trees by an equal distance. He stopped and watched. The tiny light danced and moved, as if to beckon him into the trees. It could easily have a trap, but he had always been more curious than cautious. The little light seemed gentle enough, and for some reason its behavior didn't bother him. He took a few more steps towards the trees. The light hovered for a few seconds without moving and then slowly started drifting backwards into the thick forest brush.

It moved back farther than before, floating deep into the brush. Dax took a few quick steps to get closer, but it didn't stop moving. The light moved backwards swiftly through the trees. He didn't want to let it get away without seeing it up close. There was something intriguing about it.

He stepped forward into the trees, pushing the overgrown brush aside as he entered. It was dark and dense inside. The little light had stopped a few dozen feet in front of him, seemingly waiting for him to get through the initial barrier of dense foliage. As he passed through, he refocused his attention on the light as it began its retreat again. He hurried to follow after it.

Pushing aside the thick, tall grass as he walked, he tried his best to keep up with the mysterious glowing ball. The deeper into the forest trees he got, the faster it began to move. A few times it changed direction sharply to the left or right. He struggled just to keep the golden ball in view. Just as he would think the light had disappeared, it would stop for a moment, allowing him to catch up.

Dax pushed through the dense forest for what seemed like twenty minutes before the light finally slowed down long enough for him to get close to it. He took in a few deep breaths as his jog turned into a relaxed trot. The little light rested only twelve or fifteen feet ahead. With each step he took, the shape became a little clearer. Just as he was sure he would be able to discern the features of its form, it darted backwards in a straight line, moving at a very fast pace.

Dax lunged forward with a burst of speed, trying to chase after it. His breathing grew heavy as he pushed through the thick brush. The glowing ball was moving at blinding speed, quickly widening the gap between them. He would never be able to catch it. After a few seconds it pulled away into the thick, overgrown trees ahead and was gone.

As the glowing light vanished, he was left standing alone in the high brush. The area was quite dark all around, with the bright night sky above now being his only source of light. He looked around in every direction and then back at where the light had vanished. What was he thinking? How was he going to get back to the camp with no trail and no light to see with?

Dax stared into the dark brush in front of him. He still felt the overwhelming desire to keep going. He could still feel the little light begging to be chased, but why? Had something bewitched him? He heard a noise behind him.

With one motion he drew his sword and spun around to face his stalker. Even in the low lighting he immediately recognized the familiar shape of his two best friends. Leena stood there, daggers in hand, looking at him as if he had gone completely mad.

"What in the world are you doing?" Leena demanded.

Roki stood only a few feet behind her, bent over and panting heavily, with his hammer in his right hand and his left hand clenched over his stitched-up wound. Dax felt confused.

"What are you guys doing out here?" he questioned.

"We followed you from the camp. You just took off into the trees as if you were under a spell. You wouldn't respond to our calls," Leena answered.

Dax looked back over at Roki who had a stern look of agreement on his face.

"I was chasing that glowing thing. Didn't you see it?" Dax started.

His words even sounded foolish to himself as they left his tongue.

"Never mind," he said as he turned back towards the spot where the light had disappeared.

The forest behind the thick brush in front of him still beckoned to him. He could feel the inaudible call of the glowing light.

"You must have a fever," Leena said, as if he was a lunatic.

"Leena is right, Dax. We need to get you back to camp so you can rest. You aren't thinking clearly," Roki added.

Dax knew their criticism was well placed, but it still rubbed him offensively. He didn't like being treated like a child. He continued to stare at the thick green blades of grass and vines that completely cut off his advance. It was dark and silent. Maybe he was delirious. As he was about to turn back towards them, he noticed something. Coming from behind the thick brush ahead was a dim golden glow. Was his mind still playing tricks on him?

He took a few steps forward to inspect. The glowing grew brighter the closer he got. He shot a quick glance back at his friends who were still standing there with confused looks on their faces, waiting to see what he would do next. He didn't know why he had such a strong desire to pursue the glowing ball, but he knew he couldn't stop. He moved forward again and stopped in front of the thick vines. The golden light seemed to pulse from deep inside.

A heavy swing with his sword sent the sharp blade cutting through the large green vines with surprising ease. He reached forward and pushed against the thick brush with his shoulders, forcing his way through. The sound of movement let him know that Leena close behind, fighting the tall grass as well. As he passed through the thick barrier, he was nearly blinded with a flash of brilliant golden light.

Clenching his eyes closed, he could feel the warmth pouring out from the source of the light in front of him. After a moment his eyes began to adjust, allowing his eyelids to peel open. The bright light took a moment to subside as the shape of his surroundings took form.

Chapter IX

Dax's heart nearly quit beating as he took in the awe-inspiring scenery before him. They had walked into some kind of hidden forest oasis. The short green grass was lush and vibrant. Twenty or thirty feet in front of them was a large pond with waters as clear as crystal. The transparent water flowed into the pond from multiple streams leading back up to a high waterfall in the distance. Floating through the air were tiny pixie creatures emitting a faint glowing light. Maybe one of the pixies had been what led him there?

In the middle of the giant clearing, surrounded by the flowing waters, was a large temple structure made from pure white stone. Across the front were four large stone pillars. In front of the temple a flat stone floor extended out into a set of stairs that dropped off onto another flat shelf at the water's edge.

After a few moments of his unbelief, he managed to break his gaze and glance back at his friends. Leena stood directly behind him, her dreamy, green eyes lit brightly as she stared down at the sparkling crystal waters. Roki stood off to the left looking up in awe at the high forest ceiling that completely encompassed the golden oasis. After a second, Leena spoke.

"What is this place?" she asked softly. Dax turned back around and looked over the awesome scenery.

"I have no idea," he answered.

"But I feel like something was drawing me here. There has to be a reason." With his words he started walking slowly towards the large white temple. The grass was soft under his boots and the sound of the water running down the waterfall and into the pond was pleasant to hear. The area seemed calm and safe, and despite his best attempts to be on guard, he didn't feel the least bit threatened. As he reached the water he looked down into the crystal depths. It dropped about ten feet straight down, ending with a flat bottom made of the same white stone. The water was so clear that he could easily see the small glittering fish darting all around beneath the surface.

He immediately spotted several square pillars rising up from the bottom of the lake to the surface, forming stepping stones that would allow them to cross over the water and into the temple. After studying it for a moment, he slid his sword into its sheath and glanced back at his friends for confirmation. They both returned a quick nod and waited for him to advance. He took a deep breath and hopped out onto the first platform. The stone pillar was extremely sturdy, allowing no movement whatsoever. He waited for the sound of Leena's boots leaving the ground behind him before he jumped to the next pillar. The pillars were several feet apart, but their sturdiness made it easy to advance.

After a dozen or so jumps, Dax landed firmly on the flat stone floor of the temple, half expecting to slide. However, the smooth white stone seemed to do a good job of gripping his boots. He turned back around and waited for Leena and an injured Roki to reach the temple floor before he continued. Once they both landed on the flat white stone Dax turned his attention to the middle of the large temple. He drew his sword into his right hand and raised his shield in his left. The oasis seemed tranquil but there was no way to know what waited for them inside.

A small staircase rose up in front of them, leading up to the next section of stone floor. As he reached the top step, something gave him a start. There, standing before him, were three beautiful creatures. Their soft, feminine appearance was mesmerizing. They had eyes like polished brass. Their shapely forms were covered scantily with silk robes, each one a different color. Flowing out from behind them like water, were giant ethereal wings made of pure light. Their bodies seemed to defy gravity as they floated a foot or so above the ground.

In front of the winged maidens sat three stone blocks, each one covered with arcane symbols. On top of the blocks rested heavy looking slates made of precious gemstones. The color of the gemstones seemed to coincide with the color of their robes. The leftmost slate was sapphire blue, matching the first maiden's silky sapphire robes and the circlet atop her long blonde hair. The center slate was ruby red, corresponding to the middle maiden's scarlet robes. A golden circlet sat atop her luscious curly locks of red hair. The rightmost slate was a deep green color, matching the emerald colored robe and circlet atop the dark brown hair of the third maiden.

Dax looked on, awestruck, at the miraculous scene before him. He had never seen anything as beautiful and graceful as these fair beings. The three glorious maidens remained silent as they floated effortlessly above the ground, staring at the three adventurers. Utterly terrified, Dax decided to move towards them. As he reached out his foot to take a step something stopped him. A soft voice broke the dreamy silence.

"Welcome to this sacred forest temple, heroes..." echoed the one in the middle.

Dax froze in his place, terrified. The voice didn't sound particularly threatening, but he was frightened nonetheless. He could feel Roki and Leena right next to him. He stood there motionless, waiting to see if she would say more. After another few seconds of silence he spoke back in a nervous voice.

"H-Hello, fair maidens we don't mean to intrude here. We are somewhat lost in this great forest and we stumbled onto this place by accident."

Dax let the words drift from his mouth and trail off, waiting for their response.

"Your arriving here was no accident," said the red-robed maiden in a soft voice.

"We have summoned you here."

Confusion entered Dax's mind as he tried to understand her words.

"Summoned us?" he questioned. "How do you know us? Who are you?"

The maidens on the left and right stared silently at him with gentle but somewhat mechanical expressions as the middle one spoke again.

"We are the guardians of this temple," she replied with something that resembled a faint smile.

"None can enter this sacred forest oasis unless they are summoned here by us. We were appointed long ago to watch over it, and the forest. Your race hasn't seen a creature of our lineage for hundreds of years. There is no true name for us in this realm, but you may call us fairies."

"Fairies!?" Dax choked. "I have never seen a fairy before, I've only heard stories. This is incredible."

The maiden on the left reacted quickly to his words, letting out a sigh that sounded like a cross between humor and boredom. Her brass-colored eyes seemed to glow brighter as she studied him.

"As to why we have summoned you, you will understand soon. Now, come, we have much to tell you." With her words, the red-haired fairy extended her arms down toward the stone blocks in front of them, motioning the adventurers to proceed forward. He stood there for a moment, unsure if he could trust the three powerful fairies. He knew nothing about them. What if they were falling right into a trap, he thought. He could feel his right hand tighten on the worn leather handle of his sharp short sword.

"Don't be afraid, Hero" said the middle fairy, as if she could read his thoughts. "We are incapable of harm."

With her words, he felt somehow reassured. He had no reason to trust her, but she seemed honest and gentle. He looked back at his two friends. Once he verified that they were convinced, he dropped his sword hand down to his side and stepped forward towards the stone blocks.

He could hear Roki and Leena's boots tapping the stone ground close behind him. As he reached the stone blocks, he stopped directly in front of the red robed fairy and waited for his friends to come up next to him. He looked up at the three radiant fairies hovering in front of him. Their form was the most beautiful yet terrifying thing he had ever seen. No matter how hard he tried, he couldn't resist the impulse to trace over the perfect lines of their gorgeous bodies with his eyes. Their fair bodies were flawless and attractive in every way.

"Is this form distracting?" the center fairy asked, her eyes studying his own.

"N-No," he stuttered, nervously, as the unexpected intuitiveness of the question caught him off-guard.

"Very well then," she continued.

"We have many things that we would like to tell you, heroes, but we have little time. We have summoned you to this temple for a reason and it is of grave importance."

The red robed maiden paused for a moment to make sure that everyone was listening before she continued. "Deep in the dense forest to the north of here, a dark being is rising. We can feel him gaining strength by the day. We have already started to see his dark influence spreading throughout the forest as vile and dangerous creatures have begun to rise. You have already met one of his minions, the spider queen. The dark one must be stopped before his power grows beyond control. You three must venture north from here, passing over the dark swamps and into the dense northern forests where you will face this evil being.

"Why us?" Dax blurted out impulsively.

The maiden's eyes seemed to study him thoroughly before she spoke.

"There is no one else. There is no time. If the darkness isn't stopped soon, the forest will fall. But it will not stop there. Its desire to destroy will not be quenched with the overtaking of this forest. We can sense its sinister desires. It must be defeated, and quickly. You must rise against it and fight. Should you fail, this forest, your village, and even the entire kingdom may fall. However, the choice is yours."

The maiden fell silent, patiently awaiting a response. It took a moment for her words to sink in as Dax stood there in awe of what he had heard. Could it really be true, he wondered? Would they even stand a chance against such a powerful enemy? After all, they had nearly met their match several times since they had been in the forest. He felt confused and overwhelmed by it all.

They were only adventurers, they weren't heroes. They weren't like the powerful warriors of old. Sure they had trained more than most and could hold their own in a battle, but he couldn't help but feel like this was out of their league. They could still say no. They could go back to Meadow Haven and collect on their bounty. They could live well for a while. But what if the dark enemy did come for Meadow Haven? How would anyone be able to stand against it if its powers grew even stronger? After all, the spider queen had nearly been too much for the three of them, and they were

Meadow Haven's best warriors. What would happen if even more powerful creatures descended on the village?

After a few moments of strong internal debate, he came to a decision. He knew what he was going to say, but he wanted Leena and Roki to decide for themselves. As he looked up from the ground, his eyes crossed Leena's conflicted expression. Her eyes looked worried, yet at the same time her posture seemed perfectly calm. Leena stared at him, as if trying to detect what his decision was going to be in order to help her form her own. He could tell that she weighed the risks in her mind.

He turned his attention to Roki, who was crouched down in a rigid posture, staring at the stone floor. Roki looked back up at him with a deeply conflicted look on his face before glancing off into the distance. Dax could tell that Roki had some deep concerns. Dax gave them both a few more moments to consider the proposition before finally, he spoke up.

"So what's it going to be?" he asked.

"Count me in," Leena said, without hesitation.

"Well, Roki, what about you?" Dax asked.

Roki turned towards him like he was going to speak but he didn't say anything. Dax waited for his words. After another moment of confused-looking contemplation, Roki spoke up.

"You two understand that if we do this, one or more of us may not come back? A goblin camp is one thing..." Roki asked sincerely, glancing between them.

"But, if we choose to do this, it could be the end for us."

Dax looked at his two friends with Roki's words still echoing in his mind. He understood the very real danger, but he hadn't considered that one or both of his friends might not make it. The thought of his friends dying was unbearable, especially Leena. His affections for her had grown to such a degree that he couldn't stand the thought of being without her. He had done a good job of guarding his feelings for her, but the truth was, he was in love with her. He had been for some time. Nevertheless, he wasn't willing to turn his back on such a valiant cause. It wasn't in him to run and hide. He wouldn't allow the darkness to destroy his village and everyone he knew and loved. He was going to journey through the forest to face the dark foe, live or die.

"I've made my decision," Dax said firmly, "I'm going to fight."

"I don't expect you guys to follow me. You have done enough. You can go back to town without shame," he said, looking back at Leena.

He could tell that she had considered Roki's warning as well, though it hadn't changed her mind. A part of him wished that it had.

"I've already spoken. I'm not backing out," Leena answered firmly.

Roki stared off in to the distance for a moment and then finally looked back at them.

"If this darkness threatens our home, then it must be stopped. If there is truly no one else to face it, then I guess we have no choice."

"I'm in," Roki answered.

His words gave Dax the confirmation that he was waiting for. He had already known that his friends would join him, but with so much at risk, he wanted them to be sure. He turned back toward the fairies, who still hovered silently awaiting an answer.

"We will do it," Dax answered with conviction.

The middle fairy nodded and continued.

"Good then. Go now and bathe in the inner pool. Your wounds will be soothed. Then you must rest. Your path will be perilous and your journey hard. Go now."

With her words the fairy let out a vibrant, almost musical cry and faded into swirls of light, disappearing into thin air. The other two quickly followed. Within a split second the three adventurers were standing alone at the foot of the temple.

Dax glanced around, awestruck for a second, before moving forward into the temple entrance. He could hear the others walking slowly behind him. His ears picked up on a harmonious music that seemed to grow louder and more enchanting as he walked deeper into the temple. It was dark and cool inside the temple, relaxing his stressed and tired body.

Not far inside, he caught sight of a large glowing pool of blue water. Faint sparkles and beams of light flowed around inside of it. A soft pleasant hum radiated from the pool. It beckoned him. He dropped his sword and shield to the ground behind him and untied his side bags. He pulled off his tunic and boots and placed them on the ground with the rest of his belongings, as he stepped down with one foot into the warm blue water. The smooth flowing liquid seemed to wrap around his leg and draw him in. Another step set him waist deep down into the pool.

Faint vibrations surged through his tired legs. It was invigorating. He took another step down deeper into the large pool. As the warm water touched his chest it seemed to open his airways, allowing even more of the cool damp air to flow into his lungs. He took a few slow deep breaths. His eyes dropped, and his body grew heavy. Before he realized it, his body was under the water. He could see beams of soft light swirling in front of his closed eyelids. He let his body go completely limp.

The warm water seemed to hold his body gently in place. A part of him thought for a second that he should rise to take a breath, but for some reason he knew he didn't need to. Besides, his body was nearly unresponsive. It was heavy and weak. He could feel the vibrations coursing through him. His mind even seemed to grow heavy. In a way he was afraid, yet he felt completely secure. As the last bit of strength slipped from his body, his mind drifted off. A soft golden glow swirled violently around his body and then everything went dark.

Chapter X

"Arise, Hero!"

The loud but kind voice snapped Dax from his sleep-like trance. He sat up quickly and opened his eyes. Cool, fresh air rushed into his lungs with a gasp. His heart raced to catch up. He looked around quickly. Roki and Leena were also waking up in a similar fashion. The three of them lay sprawled out across the flat stone floor directly in front of the blue pool of water.

Dax could feel his right eyebrow arch up in confusion as he realized that his pants were completely dry. How odd, he thought, as he rose to his feet. How long had they been unconscious? Immediately upon standing, he was overcome with a renewed strength in his body. His limbs were no longer heavy and tired but instead felt full of energy and vigor. He clenched his fist hard and smiled with delight at the returned sturdiness surging within his full muscles. The pool had seemed to heal his wound as well. He could barely believe it.

He glanced over at his friends who were now also rising to their feet. The expressions on their faces seemed to indicate they were feeling a similar sentiment. Roki pulled back his torn tunic with a gasp. His deep wound had been completely healed, without as much as a scratch remaining. Dax reached down and grabbed his gear from the cold stone floor and began replacing each item, when the voice echoed again.

"Come heroes," the voice demanded.

He couldn't tell if the voice was spoken aloud or only inside his head. He finished strapping his shield onto his back and turned around as his friends trailed behind. As soon as he stepped outside of the dark inner temple, his eyes immediately caught sight of the three mesmerizing figures once again. Behind the stone altars their ethereal bodies hovered weightlessly, glowing with energy. Dax strode forward and stopped in front of the altars as the red clad fairy began to speak.

"Now that your bodies are rejuvenated, you must continue your journey. But first, we will grant you a gift. Place your weapons upon these stones, heroes, and we will bestow upon each one of them an enchantment."

With a small amount of hesitation, Dax drew his shiny short sword from its sheath and placed it slowly onto the glowing slate atop the white stone altar. He glanced over as Roki and Leena did the same. After a moment the center fairy looked up towards the sky and opened her mouth, letting out a loud thundering cry.

Dax immediately dropped to his knees as the ground beneath him started to shake. Each fairy began to glow and pulse with a bright energy that matched the color of their robes. He could hardly make out the shapes before him as the three beings began to shake violently. He could feel the energy vibrating through the air all around him. Strong gusts of wind whipped through the air in a wide circular motion.

Within a few seconds the light emitting from the fairies grew too bright to see any figures. Dax put his right arm up over his face to shield from the brightness. He couldn't make out anything and the strong wind was pushing him all over the place. He dropped down low to the ground to try and stabilize his body while quickly looking over to see if Leena was having the same troubles. He could almost make out her dark colored clothing. Suddenly a deafening crack of thunder echoed out above them and a mighty gust of wind shot downwards, pushing him hard into the stone floor.

The strong wind gust coincided with a burst of blinding light that was so bright it caused his eyes to forcefully slam shut. As soon as the light struck the area in front of him, a loud humming noise rang out and then slowly diminished, taking the bright light with it. After the light was gone, everything fell silent and calm. He could feel the cold smooth stone still pressing against his face.

Once his bewilderment wore off, Dax cracked open his eyes and looked around. He could see Leena plainly, lying on the ground a few feet away. Her eyes were opened and immediately locked gaze with his. He could tell that she enjoyed the event as an awkward smile formed on her face. He looked back down at the ground and let out a relieved sigh, pushing himself onto his hands and feet.

He stood up slowly, somewhat dazed. After a quick glance at Roki let him know that they were all okay, Dax continued forward to where the fairies had been. He could see no trace of the ethereal creatures, but his eyes grew wide as he gazed upon the stone pillars, their weapons still glowing from the fairies' enchantments. The glow faded slowly as they approached the pillars.

After a few seconds of silence, Dax cautiously grabbed on to his shiny short sword and brought it up to eye level. It looked much the same as before, though something did seem different about it. It seemed lighter than before, and shinier. The silver of the blade looked purer, almost white in color. But still, the changes seemed subtle at best. He gripped the handle firmly and took a few small swipes through the air. It sliced through the air smoothly with a nice humming sound. After swinging it a few times, he could tell that it was definitely lighter. The speed at which the razor-sharp blade now cut through the air would make his attacks even more deadly. He couldn't wait to try it out on something.

Roki moving his heavy hammer around grabbed his attention. He was looking at the steel in much the same way as Dax had. Roki's large arms moved the massive hammer back and forth, as if testing its weight. Dax noticed immediately that the heavy hammer seemed much lighter and easier for Roki to maneuver.

Roki smiled as he swung the hammer from side to side, obviously enjoying its increased quality. Dax then turned his attention to Leena. She was standing with her bow hand extended, testing the string's integrity with her other hand. She drew back a few times quickly and then slowly dropped the string back down. Dax could see her tracing over the lines of the wood with her eyes, examining every detail to make sure that the weapon hadn't been compromised. After a moment, Leena looked up with a satisfied look on her face.

"What do you think?" Dax asked.

"It seems different somehow," Leena answered. "It almost feels lighter than before, maybe stronger too." Before they could inspect the enchanted weapons any more the fairy's voice interrupted.

"You haven't much time heroes. The power of our enemy grows," the voice warned. Dax looked around quickly to see where the voice was coming from but there was nothing. Again, it echoed.

"We have opened the path in front of you. From here you will journey through the forest swamps and into the dense heart of the forest. Be vigilant, be strong and be careful. Good luck heroes. May the divine one watch over you all." The soft voice trailed off as he peered across the hidden forest oasis towards the other side of the enclosure.

Dax quickly spotted an area where the trees separated, revealing a path out. "That must be the path out of here," he said, pointing towards the parted trees. Roki and Leena looked over at the path and nodded in agreement. Dax slid his newly enchanted sword into its sheath and started across the temple towards the exit. As he walked, he savored the lush beautiful scenery and cool fresh air. The air flowed into his lungs in slow deep breaths, giving him a sense of peace and stillness.

Dax crossed quickly over more stepping stones to the other side of the lake and moved across the field of grass until he reached the exit. A small parting of the large tree trunks and stone boulders revealed their way out. It was dark on the other side. He couldn't see anything down the path.

"This is it guys. No turning back now. Are you ready?" he questioned.

"Ready" Roki and Leena answered simultaneously.

"Okay then. Let's move."

With his words, Dax bent down slightly and stepped through the opening into the dark and narrow passage. He could barely see in front of him as he inched forwards. After a few feet he came upon a wall of twisted black blanches and brush. He drew his sword and took a few hard swipes. The blade cut through the hardened branches with ease, like a knife through warm butter. The branches fell to the ground with a light thud and he stepped forward through the opening.

On the other side, the area immediately opened back up into the familiar forest, though the new area was much more eerie. Echoes and creeks could be heard from all directions, and the atmosphere felt strange. Dax kept his sword drawn high and moved forward. Occasionally, his eyes would catch a quick movement off in the shadows of the trees, but if there were creatures around them, they didn't seem to want a fight. The further he moved into the forest ahead, the darker it seemed to grow. Before long, he found himself barely able to see. He stretched out his sword in front of him so that he would be ready in case of an attack. His eyes widened as something strange caught him off guard. It was most peculiar. The shiny blade of his newly-enchanted sword began to glow with a warm pinkish-red light, illuminating the area all around them. The light that it produced seemed to brighten even the dark crevices and far shadows. He could see everything around him plainly for at least a hundred-foot radius. The bright light gave him much more confidence as he walked forward, deeper into the forest.

As he pushed ahead through the dark forest, he still couldn't believe all that had happened. It felt like days had passed since they first entered the forest in search of the goblin bandits. He thought back over the ambush inside of the goblin hideout and the leader's surprise attack that had gotten the better of him. He thought about the forest maze and the mysterious fog that had separated them, leading to the battle with the giant spiders. He thought about the frightening clash with the spider queen that had nearly claimed all of their lives. They had come so far, and prevailed through so much danger, but he couldn't help but question their efforts. Had they survived because they continued to grow stronger and more skillful, or was it just a fluke that their hearts still beat in their chests? Would their determination and will to survive keep them moving forward, or would their luck eventually run out? When would their skills fail them? There was no sure way to know.

He continued ahead for what seemed like at least an hour and still hadn't come across any definite signs of life. Most of the previous sounds and movements had faded away completely. There were no creatures stirring, or insects chirping. The now-quiet forest had seemed to become completely devoid of life. It seemed strange to him, but it was easier not having to pay attention to every sound. Besides, the fewer things they had to fight off, the better.

The light from his sword and absence of distractions let them gain ground easily. After nearly another hour, the air began to grow cooler. The large, twisted, tree trunks started to thin out and become even scarcer, with one every twenty or thirty feet. The ground had grown soft and wet. Soon a light fog rose up into the air. As they pressed on, the fog quickly thickened, stopping visibility at about a dozen feet.

Being cautious, he slowed his advancement considerably. As the fog thickened, the red light from his sword seemed to brighten the white mist, making it harder to see. As soon as the thought crossed his mind, the glow of his sword began to fade, almost as if it reacted to his desire. As the bright glow faded, the view ahead became a little clearer. The wet brown dirt in front of him grew narrow as shallow looking pools of dark-colored water closed in on the sides.

"The path is narrow up ahead, we should be careful," Dax whispered behind him.

As he stepped forward onto the wet ground, he could feel the slipperiness of it beneath his hard boots. He took care to set his footing each time before moving forward. A faint moonlight seemed to cast a light glow overhead, reflecting slightly off the blackish water on either side. Dax glanced through the mist and out over the waters to his left. It was impossible to tell how far the water stretched or even how deep it was. All he could see was a dull reflection of light atop calm black ripples. He focused ahead and continued walking slowly.

After a hundred feet or so, he came to a stop and listened. He could hear a constant quiet whipping of water against a hard surface. *THOOP, THOOP, THOOP.* It sounded quite normal for a body of water, but it did let him know that there was at least some movement from either one direction or the other.

Dax staggered across the slippery ground again, clenching his sword tightly in his right hand, ready for anything that might lunge out at him unexpectedly. Another fifty feet and the path opened back up a little bit wider, making it easier to walk ahead. The ground was wetter there, but the dirt was softer, making it much less slippery. As he walked, he kept his eyes on the water. It had risen higher than before, making it almost level with the ground. The boundary between the two was hard to distinguish.

He kept a close watch on either side and began to increase his speed a little when he felt Leena's small hand grip his shoulder tightly. He stopped immediately and waited. The way Leena had gripped his shoulder told him that she was alarmed. Maybe she had heard something. He could feel Leena move in close behind him and drop down. He slowly crouched down and waited for her to speak. After a moment of her being silent, he spoke up.

"What is it, Leena?" he asked.

"Shh," Leena answered sharply. Dax tried to be patient, but he could feel his heart beat a little faster with anticipation.

"Listen," Leena whispered, her grip tightening slightly. Dax focused hard and listened. He could only hear the hum of silence and the faint mechanical thumping of water against an unseen bank. There was nothing else. Suddenly he heard it. It was ever-so-quiet. It was the sound of water rolling as something moved beneath the surface. It wasn't close enough to the surface to make a splash, but it was movement enough to make a sound.

"What was that?" he whispered frantically.

"I'm not sure, but something is definitely alive down there. I don't know about you, but I don't want to stick around and find out what it is," Leena answered with a serious tone. Dax waved his sword over his shoulder, signaling his friends to follow, as he stood up and paced ahead quickly, trying to walk as quietly as possible. He rushed forward into the mist, being able to see just far enough ahead to make sure his path was clear. The reassuring sound of his friends' light footsteps behind let him know to keep moving.

Chapter XI

Despite the compromised visibility and unknown terrain, they were advancing quickly. The sooner they got away from the dark water, the better. Dax had an uneasy feeling about the place. He pushed ahead into a light sprint as the mist seemed to thin out a bit, making it easier to see ahead. His boots sank into the soft mud as he covered the ground. After a short while, he came to a stop. He could see just far enough out in front of him to tell that the water completely covered the path. He held his sword up high and hoped for more light. With only a thought, the blade began to glow brightly once again, giving him just enough light to see what he needed to.

"The path ahead is covered in water. It goes under for about a hundred feet and then rises back up onto land. I can't see anything past that," he whispered to the others.

"We have no choice, we can't stay here," Leena replied.

"Agreed," muttered Roki from the back.

"Just stay close to each other. We have no idea how deep it is or what's in there," Dax said as he stepped down into the dark water.

Immediately he could feel the cold water soak into his leather boots and pant legs as his heavy boots sank deep into the mud underneath. He took a slow deep breath and waded in further. As the water hit his waist, he breathed in sharply with a gasp. It was colder than he had realized. It also felt somewhat slimy.

He forced another breath and stepped out further until he was up to his shoulders in the slimy cold water. Leena's hand on his shoulder let him know she was close behind. He continued moving, pulling his feet out from the soft mud and stepping forward again. It didn't seem to grow any deeper as he walked, but it was bitterly cold, which seemed to help quicken his advance. Step after step, he kept trudging ahead, covering nearly thirty feet in just a few seconds. As he was about to take his next step, something caused him to pause. It was a sound. Just like the rolling water from before, only this time, it was much closer.

He could feel the underwater wave that the movement created. His heart began to beat faster. He could feel Leena's grip tighten on his shoulder. She had felt it too. There was something below the surface. They had to get to the other side as quickly as possible. There was no time for subtlety.

"Run!" Dax shouted as he exploded from the soft ground underneath.

He rushed forward with everything, trying desperately to gain speed. He covered another thirty or so feet, moving through the mud and water with every ounce of strength. Light splashing behind let him know that his friends were doing a good job at keeping up. They were almost there. Dax felt a big wave of water pass in front of him, pushing him back a foot or two, followed by the sound of rushing water. Whatever it was, it was right on them. There was no getting away.

He readied his sword hand and scanned the dark waters with his eyes, ready to strike at any signs of movement. Out of nowhere a large crash of water rang out from behind, followed by a giant wave. The sheer force of the wave sent him flying forward twenty or thirty feet. The current was far too strong to fight against. As the current subsided he found himself at the base of the water. He could still feel Leena's hand gripping his shoulder. He reached around, grabbed her hand and then pushed forward.

Two or three steps and they rose up out of the muddy, cold water and onto dryer land. He turned around quickly as soon as he was out of the water and looked back. Roki was just stepping up out of the water behind them. Leena already had an arrow at full draw, scanning the waters. They stood there, staring down into the dark slimy liquid, waiting for their foe to reveal itself. The water was still and quiet. After a few moments of silence, Dax finally spoke up.

"Okay, let's move," he said quickly.

As he turned around and started to move, suddenly he heard a loud splash. He turned back just in time to see a large dark object flash in front of them and slam into Roki, throwing him back into the dark pond.

"Roki!" he shouted.

Leena was diligently searching the waters looking for anything to fire an arrow at. He ran quickly to the edge of the water and held his sword up high. Immediately the bright light illuminated the top of the blackish colored lake. The water was much too dark to see down into but the ripples from Roki's impact were still bouncing across the surface. Dax stared hard and listened. It was silent. Roki had to be under there somewhere.

Dax froze in place nervously for a few more seconds, waiting for any sign of his friend but he quickly realized it wasn't coming. He had no choice. He would have to jump in after him. Dax stood up and took a few steps back, focusing on the spot where Roki had gone under the water. Without hesitation, he took in a deep breath and charged forward, plunging headfirst into the black water.

The complete submersion of his dry head into the cold water sent a quick shiver down Dax's spine. He couldn't see anything in front of him, but he swam deeper and deeper downwards, hoping Roki was somewhere near the bottom. After a few seconds of swimming downwards, he realized that the water was much deeper than he had originally thought.

He felt around for any sign of his friend. Slimy moss and soft weeds ran through his fingers as his hands moved through the water. Just then something clamped down hard onto his forearm, making him nearly swing his sword at it before he realized that it was a familiar touch. It was Roki's hand grabbing at him. He could tell from the embrace that Roki was alive but frantic at best.

Dax quickly felt upwards until his hand met Roki's shoulder. He grabbed on tight and pulled, but it was no use. Something held Roki's body firmly in place. He had to free him quickly before they both ran out of air. He brushed his hand along Roki's shoulders and chest. Suddenly his hand froze in place as it dropped onto the massive object that was holding Roki. It was wrapped tightly around his midsection. Dax felt his eyes widen and his heart flutter in panic as his hand slid along the smooth scaly object. He could feel it moving, tightening...reacting. It was alive.

There was no time to devise a strategy. He had to free Roki fast. Dax pulled his sword quickly upwards and stabbed down hard, piercing easily into the creature's thick skin. The creature's lightning fast reaction to the attack caused it to release Roki and jerk towards Dax. It slammed into his chest like an explosion, forcing every bit of air out of his lungs.

The impact sent him hurling backwards. Immediately his entire body began to pound with pain. He struggled to regain control, but his sense of direction had disappeared, and was now replaced with a feeling of dizziness. He had to get to the surface. He could feel his lungs crying out for air. His feet kicked hard against the water, and his arms flailed, but before he could move he felt a quick rush of water as the smooth, scaly skin slid across his body. It circled quickly around his torso and clamped down.

The strength of the creature's grip was unfathomable. Dax felt an immediate flood of searing pain streak through his body, his bones and flesh buckling inwards as it tightened down. The pain was beyond words. He could feel the tiny blood vessels bursting in his eyes as the pressure rose higher. He couldn't move or even scream. He wondered if Roki had gotten away or if his friend was enduring a similar fate.

Just as he was sure his body would give out, the grip lessened slightly, and he felt himself rush upwards through the water. As his face broke the surface of the water, the creature's grip had loosened just enough for him to inhale a short burst of cool air before the death lock returned. With the small bit of air in his constricted lungs he let out a violent but muffled scream as the pressure forced the air back out.

He tried to pull in another tiny breath, but the grip was too tight. As the agonizing pain shot through his chest, he glanced around in a panic. His body was suspended a good eight feet above the water's surface, facing down at his two friends. Roki was just climbing back up out of the water onto dry land and Leena was staring up at him with a horrified look on her face, with her bow still drawn.

He could see the panic and concentration on Leena's face as she searched for the shot. But there was no time left. He could feel his bones and insides buckling beneath the pressure. He would be gone in a matter of seconds. Everything seemed to slow to a crawl as he watched Leena's fingers drop gracefully from the bowstring, sending a thin shafted arrow streaming from the bow. It tore through the air and collided with the creature's thick scaly skin, only inches away from his chest torso.

As the arrow hit its mark, the creature jolted violently, immediately loosening its grip. Searing pain tore through his chest cavity as he dropped back down into the water with a splash. The impact pushed him several feet below the surface. The throbbing pain in his body was horrendous but he quickly swam with all his strength to the surface.

He gasped hard as the cool air filled his battered lungs and abdomen. Pain streaked across his chest and ribcage. As he began to exhale, he let out an uncontrollable cry of agony and started swimming hastily towards land. Something off to his left caught his eye as it rose sharply above the water and then slammed back down towards him, causing a large splash. A wall of water collided with his face, nearly blinding him. *THWAP*, *THWAP*. He could hear Leena firing more arrows in rapid succession. He kept his head down and kept swimming.

Just then something else caught his attention. Deep beneath the water he could see a bright pink glow. Something was beneath him, but what was it? He quickly recognized its familiar glow. It was his sword. It had been knocked free from his hand at some point, and it was now resting at the bottom of the lake. He had to get it, and fast.

With a deep painful breath in, he turned and dived downwards, kicking his feet and arms. Deeper and deeper he swam towards the glowing light. It was harder to hold his breath with his damaged torso, but he had to get his weapon back. Without it he was completely defenseless.

With a final push, he reached down and grabbed ahold of the smooth wooden handle. As he drew the sword from the ground something exploded out of the shadows towards him. He barely caught a glimpse of the dark creature's oval shaped head and large beady eyes as it lunged for him. Without even a second to aim, he swung his sword wildly towards the creature. The blade struck against its body, slicing into its thick skin. He quickly rolled to the side and pushed upwards again towards the surface. Another painful breath of cool air entered his lungs as his head rose above the water. The panic-stricken voices of his two friends immediately rang out.

"Dax!" they screamed simultaneously.

He paddled frantically towards them. As he reached the edge of the water, Roki grabbed on to his hand and pulled him up. With a final lunge, he rose up out of the water and onto the dry ground. He took in a large gasp of air, followed by several more. The quick breathes didn't seem to quench his body's thirst for more oxygen.

As Dax regained his calm, he turned around, ready to face the creature's next attacks. He investigated the dark black water with concentration. Where was it? The only movement present was the faint rippling of waves across the surface. He watched and waited, breathing heavily. It could've been anywhere.

Just then a wall of water exploded towards them as something lunged up high above the surface. As the water splashed down onto the ground, Dax looked up in horror at the image before him. The serpent's body was nearly as wide as he was tall, long and slender. It rose up fifteen or twenty feet above the water. On top of its long, smooth, scaly body rested a narrow, cunning looking head. It had large, dark, beady, soul-less eyes. Their depth seemed to hold him in place like some sort of death gaze.

He couldn't move. His heart pounded as he looked up at the giant water serpent. All at once the creature threw its jaws open, revealing two long razor-sharp fangs. It let out a chaotic squeal and lunged forward with blinding speed straight toward him. He felt the nervousness in his hand as it clenched tightly around the handle of his sword.

As the serpent's massive jaws nearly reached him, an unexpected swing of Roki's massive hammer slammed into the left side of the serpent's body, causing it to move to the side. It slithered backwards quickly and lunged at Roki. Leena's bowstring rang out as she sent two arrows barreling into the creature's head. It hissed loudly and slammed its heavy tail into the water beside Leena, sending a large wave of water crashing toward her. The force knocked her back several feet as the water splashed to the ground.

The large serpent turned back to Roki and threw its massive jaws open with another hiss. Dax rushed in quickly to defend his friend, but his advance was met by the serpent's hard tail. The collision forced the breath out of his lungs again as he went flying backwards.

More pain jolted through his upper body as his body slammed into the ground. He struggled to stand up quickly. Through disoriented eyes, he looked up just in time to see the cunning serpent lunge right towards him, fangs bared. He dropped down and rolled backwards, bringing his sword up right underneath of the creature's head. With all his strength he shoved the sharp blade upwards forcefully.

The blade sliced through the tough scales with ease, passing cleanly through its bottom jaw and the roof of its mouth. The creature collided hard with his body, sending him tumbling backwards. Once his body stopped moving, he quickly rolled back onto his feet and looked up. The shiny sword was still stuck through the bottom of the serpent's jaw and up into its head.

More chaotic squeals followed as the creature's body spasms sent its head slamming into the ground here and there. Leena quickly fired a few more arrows into the flailing beast, causing even more violent thrashing.

After a few moments, the flailing lessened into a squirm and then eventually into a twitch. As the twitching began to subside, Dax walked up and gripped the sword handle tightly, drawing it out of the serpent. As the blade left the creature's head a smooth flow of dark red blood followed. The twitching of the creature's body made him uneasy.

He jumped up, and with another forceful attack, drove the sharp blade downwards through the top of the creature's large, thick skull. Immediately the serpent's tail began to thrash around violently. After a few seconds, the flailing stopped and the beast fell motionless. Dax jerked the sharp blade out and stood there for a moment breathing heavily, replaying the last few minutes in his mind. It had happened so fast. Strong pains still shot down his chest and ribcage with every breath. He put his hand against his ribs and applied some pressure to help ease the pain. After a moment, he looked over at his friends.

"Are you okay?" Roki asked, in a worried tone. Dax looked down at his body and then back up.

"I'm a little banged up, but I'll be fine," he answered, short of breath. Roki stepped forward and put his hand on his shoulder.

"Thanks for the save," Roki said, earnestly. Dax forced a smile.

"Don't mention it," he replied. Pain streaked across his right side as the muscles around his diaphragm contracted. After a brief coughing fit, which caused even more pain, he looked to Leena.

"And thank you for that well-placed arrow. I wasn't sure how I was going to get out of that one." Leena looked back at him with affectionate eyes. "I'm just glad you're okay, Dax," she said, her bright red lips curling upwards Even through his agony he enjoyed seeing her attractive smile. It seemed to make the pain a little easier to bear.

All at once a bright explosion of light surrounded the creature as brilliant, blue flames engulfed its lifeless body. The flame burned fast and hot as the serpent's body quickly disintegrated into ash. After only a few seconds the creature's body was gone. Just like before, the mood of the area seemed to quickly change. The mist thinned out and fell to the ground. The darkened sky above seemed to lighten up, and the dark waters appeared lighter and less eerie. It seemed as though the creature's death released the area from the dark influence.

Dax glanced back at Roki and Leena who both stood in silence, staring at the spot where the giant serpent had been. He could tell that they were just as confused and uneasy as he was. What was behind all of it, he wondered? He had a feeling they would find out soon enough. After another moment or two, he spoke up.

"I suppose we should get moving. I don't want to wait around to see if more of those things show up." He took the lead again and continued forward down the dark path. As he walked, the cool air hitting his wet body sent shivers down his spine. His whole upper body throbbed. After two or three hundred feet the dark water began to roll back away from the path on either side, being replaced by rugged looking knee-high brush.

He held his sword up high to light the path. He could still see the reflections bouncing off of the water's surface, but it was much farther away from the path than before. Moving away from the water made him feel much more comfortable.

He trudged through the mud and brush for what felt like hours before the sky above started to lighten up into a dim yellow hue, making the area around them more visible. As the area brightened, he looked ahead at the scenery. They had entered into bland, rugged-looking swamplands. All across the swamps were large ponds of brown water, separated by patches of muddy brown dirt and tall grass. Most of the ponds looked about knee high, with a few deeper looking ones here and there.

Scattered across the land, large dark trees raised high into the sky. The treetops were mostly bare for the first time since they entered the forest, but a humid haze prevented them from seeing too far into the sky. The humidity in the air made it impossible to see more than two or three hundred feet ahead. With the area brightened, at least they would be able to defend against another attack.

He moved forward over the moist dirt path with caution. He had never ventured through swamplands before. It was a different feeling. It was nice to be able to see around them, but he couldn't help but feel like an easy target.

They travelled for another hour or so before coming to an area where the small pools of water all but disappeared. The ground leveled out, with the dark brown mud fading into soft green grass. In front of them a way, in the middle of a clearing of damp grass, grew a large tree. It looked to be the perfect shelter for a quick rest. It would give them some time to catch their breath and regroup.

He motioned over his shoulder for the others to advance. Roki and Leena moved forward ahead of him towards the giant tree while he glanced around quickly to make sure the area was secure. It seemed fairly calm. After he was sure they were alone, he quickly joined his friends. Roki had already dropped his heavy hammer down to the ground and sat atop a small round boulder, drinking water from a wineskin. Leena stood calmly, propped against the sturdy tree trunk with her eyes closed.

Dax moved in near the tree and dropped into a sitting position. He reached behind his back and pulled on the leather straps that held his shield in place. As the straps loosened, the small round shield dropped to the ground. He placed his sword on top of it and dropped the leather sheath from his back. He scooted his back up against the tree and relaxed. It felt good to sit. His muscles and bones ached from his injuries but not nearly as bad as before. His eyes were heavy. He felt like he could pass out at any point. He didn't have time to rest, but maybe he would just rest his eyes for a minute.

Chapter XII

Roki gazed back over the dull looking swamplands, trying not to feel uneasy. It all just looked so unnatural to him. Over the years he had grown partial to Meadow Haven's fresh green grass, cool crisp air, and bright blue skies. He had never seen swampland before. The dark shades of brown and grey were melancholy at best. The place made him feel tired and depressed.

He looked over at his friend Dax, who sat beneath the giant tree sleeping. Having been caught in the swamp serpent's death grip as well, he knew that Dax must've been in a considerable amount of pain. Dax would need all the rest he could get. After all, he had taken the brunt of the serpent's attack. The injuries would have been his own, had Dax not intervened. He was lucky to have such a brave friend. His attention returned as Leena came walking up holding a small bird in one hand and her bow in the other.

"How's he doing?" she asked.

Roki glanced over at his sleeping friend and then back at Leena.

"He's Okay. He just needs some rest. I imagine he has at least a broken rib or two, if not worse," he answered.

"We can let him sleep for a while. I will start a fire and get some food going," Leena said as she carried the limp bird a few feet away.

Hot food sounded great to him. Every bit of bread and cheese that they were carrying with them had been soaked by the slimy swamp water. He didn't know how she had managed to find anything alive in the desolate swamps, but he was glad that she had. His stomach had been growling for hours.

Roki looked down at his newly-enchanted hammer. It seemed to almost sparkle faintly in the light. It called into his mind everything that had happened. It was hard to believe that the fairies had entrusted them with such an important mission. What if they failed? What if they weren't strong enough? A part of him wondered if they would ever see their quiet, peaceful, town again. What had Dax managed to get the three of them into? Roki tried to fight against the small feeling of resentment over the whole thing. It just seemed like Dax, as good of a fighter as he was, was always a little eager to head into uncertain danger. He never seemed to stop and consider the possible outcomes, or who might have to pay the price. Roki took a few more sips off the small water bag and dropped it back down to his side before turning towards Leena.

"What do you think of all this?" he asked, hoping she would say something that might ease his anxious mind.

"All of what?" she responded as she struck a spark into the soft pile of kindling, igniting it into a small flame.

"I mean all of it, the fairies, the dangerous creatures, the dark magic," he continued.

Leena's plump red lips parted as she blew into the struggling flame. Her long dark hair draped over her left shoulder. He respected Leena as a friend, as a warrior, but sometimes he couldn't help but admire her feminine traits.

"I'm not sure what to think," Leena started. "It all seems a little unreal to me."

She stared into the small red flames for a moment before continuing.

"We've spent so much time training and exploring in the forest. In that time, our skills have grown so much, but I can't help but wonder if it's enough. We have no idea what lies ahead or what's waiting for us in the heart of the forest. The fairies seem to think we have a chance, but how many close calls have we had in only a short time? I just hope we make it out of this in one piece."

Roki thought about her words as he peered into the now growing campfire. At least he wasn't the only one who had doubts. He was used to Leena always being so confident and precise. It was nice to see her vulnerable side occasionally. She seemed different since her run-in with the spiders. He didn't know if it was good or bad, but he worried that the experience had affected her confidence. He felt the need to reassure her.

"We'll be okay, Leena," he said. "We always find a way to pull through."

His words seemed to at least comfort her, regardless of if she believed them or not. The truth was, he didn't know what dangers lay ahead. He had all the same doubts as she did, and more. Thinking about it made him nervous, but he wasn't going to let it eat at him. He had to stay strong for his friends.

He watched as Leena prepared the small bird with her razor-sharp dagger and began roasting it over the campfire. The aroma of the bird's charred skin immediately made his stomach rumble and reminded him of the meals his mother would make. He missed his home. He missed his bed, even if it was hard as a rock.

After the meat was ready, Leena pulled it apart and handed him a portion. He tossed some into his mouth and chewed. The meat was moist and delicious. It was exactly what his body needed. He devoured the large portion in only a few seconds, leaving his stomach satisfied.

"Thank you, Leena," he said, as he took another drink from his wineskin.

"No problem," she said, "I didn't think hunting would be very easy with a giant hammer."

He laughed. It was nice to hear her joke after everything.

"I suppose it's time to wake him?" Leena asked.

Roki looked over at his tired and battered friend.

"Let's give him a few more minutes," he answered.

After some more time had gone by, Leena grabbed some of the meat and walked over to Dax. She bent down and slowly touched his shoulder. His eyes opened with a jolt and his hand reached down for his sword. Dax quickly recognized Leena and relaxed his arm. Roki watched as she handed Dax the freshly roasted meat. He could see the smile form on Dax's face and the look in his eyes as she kneeled beside him.

Roki could see the affection. He had been aware of Dax's feelings toward Leena for quite some time, but only recently did he start to notice that she shared the same feelings. The locked gazes, the faint smiles... the awkward moments. He was no fool. He could see the affection brewing between them. He tried not to let it bother him. They were his friends and their feelings for each other wouldn't change that, even if he himself was also captivated by her. He was content just being a friend and nothing more.

After a half hour or so of resting, it was time to press on. Roki stood up from his cozy rock and grabbed ahold of his hammer. It seemed much lighter than it had before. Maybe it was from the fairies' enchantment, or maybe it was just because his strength had grown. He couldn't tell. He threw the heavy hammer onto his shoulder and waited for Dax to finish strapping his gear back on. Leena had already thrown some water over the small campfire and was ready to move. Roki moved in behind Dax and Leena as they left the shade of the large tree and headed out towards the grass-covered flatlands.

They moved across the flat ground easily, allowing them to cover a large distance in a short amount of time. He could tell by Dax's quickened pace that he must've been feeling better. Roki tried to keep up, while at the same time watching to the sides for danger. There didn't seem to be any signs of life, besides a few scurrying scavengers. He still had an uneasy feeling about the place, but at least the short grass was far more pleasant than the dull muddy ponds. The thin grey haze had thinned out to a point where he could start to see the pale blue sky far above. A short, cool, breeze made him instantly aware that a thin line of sweat that had begun to form on his forehead.

After an easy yet somewhat lengthy trek over the grassland, Dax's voice caught his attention.

"There," Dax said excitedly, pointing into the distance ahead, "I can see the tree line."

Roki took a few steps up and peered through the thin, misty haze at the vague scenery far ahead. He could see the dense wall of dark tall trees a couple thousand feet ahead. They were getting closer to their destination. They had passed through the ugly swamps, over the flatland, and now closed in towards the deepest part of the forest. Roki couldn't wait to get back into the cover of the thick trees where he would feel more protected.

After a moment of studying the area, Dax gave the group a motion to advance. They moved quickly across the dry flat grass towards the distant trees. Roki came to an abrupt halt as something up ahead caused Leena to stop suddenly. He watched as she crouched down low and studied the area far ahead of them. As soon as Dax noticed that Roki and Leena weren't following, he stopped and looked back at them with a confused look. Roki took a few steps forward and kneeled beside Leena. He quickly scanned over the path up ahead to see what alarmed her. He didn't see anything at all. The large tree trunks, high brush, and dark tree line ahead were completely still. There was barely even a faint breeze. After a few moments Leena slowly dropped her bow string back down. She stared off into the distance for another moment before speaking.

"Sorry..." she said in a slow, odd manner. "I thought I saw something moving up ahead in the trees."

Roki looked again into the dark tree line. It strained his eyes just to try and pick out the various large branches. Between the thin haze in the air and the considerable distance, it was difficult to see anything. But still, it looked silent from what he could tell.

"What is it?" Dax questioned.

Leena still stared ahead with a concentrated look.

"N-nothing... it was nothing," Leena stuttered.

"Are you sure?" Dax pushed.

"It was just a false alarm. We should keep moving," she answered, a little more confidently.

With her words, she stood up and started walking again. Dax turned around and shrugged it off, moving to take the lead again. He seemed more cautious than before, walking a bit slower. Leena was quiet. She seemed distracted. Roki couldn't help but think maybe she was getting a little delirious from the injuries and lack of sleep. He wasn't feeling that great himself.

After walking further, as the familiar view of the forest trees returned, Leena dropped down, drawing an arrow from her quiver. She pulled back on the bow string slowly. He could see her head darting around as she searched the tree line far ahead. Her aim moved swiftly here and there, as if she was tracking several different targets at once. He could see her breathing heavily. He focused intently on the dense tree line up ahead, trying to pinpoint any sign of movement. There was nothing. Everything was still and quiet. What was she seeing? He quickly moved in closer to her and placed his hand on her shoulder. The embrace instantly caused a strong flinching reflex. Leena jolted her head toward him with a nervous glare. His familiar face seemed to calm her down, but she still looked deeply concerned. Something was wrong with her.

"What is it, Leena?" he questioned.

Leena stared at him for a moment and then returned her gaze to the forest.

"I thought my eyes had been playing tricks on me," she answered quietly, almost whispering. "But I was wrong. There is something up there in the trees."

Dax shot a quick glance back at him and then back down at Leena.

"Are you positive?" Dax questioned, his tone hinting at his disbelief.

After a second or two, Leena responded. "I'm sure, I can see the movement."

"What is it?" Dax questioned as he peered intently into the distant trees.

"I can't quite make it out," Leena said quietly. "But it's big."

She jerked her aim a little farther to the left.

"Wait..." she said nervously.

"There's more than one."

Suddenly she let out a gasp as her eyes widened.

"Oh no!" she cried.

But before she could issue her warning, a roaring commotion rang out ahead. Roki's heart felt as if it dropped into the bottom of his stomach as he watched the massive grey-skinned creatures pour out of the dense forest far ahead. Leena was right. There was more than one. There had to be at least two dozen of the creatures running violently towards them, with more still pouring out behind the others.

Finally, Leena managed to sound off her dire warning.

"Orcs!!" she cried loudly, as she pointed ahead at the advancing group of massive orcs.

More and more of them appeared every second. The large creatures poured out of the dense trees like a pile of salt through a braided fishing net. Their heavy bodies and large feet pounded into the ground as they rushed forward, only a thousand or so feet ahead. Within only a few seconds time, the group of a dozen orcs had grown into a large horde. Roki looked on in horror at the sheer size of the advancing army. They were closing the distance quickly. The horde would be upon them in under a minute. They had to form a strategy.

Before he could get any words out, Dax spoke up in a loud voice.

"Alright, listen, there's no retreating from this, we can't outrun them, and there's no time to plan an attack. We can't advance against an army of that size. There must be a hundred of them. We must stay in a tight group and watch each other's backs like. If we let our defense down for even a second, we're dead."

Dax looked back him and then at Leena, motioning towards the army.

"Leena, you fire as many arrows as possible into that horde before it gets here. If we can reduce their numbers before they even get to us we might stand a chance. Roki, you have the biggest weapon here, try to make every attack count and take out as many of those things as you can."

Dax's voice went silent for a moment.

"Leena, anything we need to know about fighting orcs?" he questioned.

Roki knew why he asked the question. She was the only one of them who had seen an orc in real life. The Orcs and Woodlings were the gravest of enemies. From a young age the children of her clan were taught to fight and defend themselves in case of an orc attack. Once, when she was only a child, an orc army had invaded her village, slaughtering many of her people. She hated the vile creatures.

After a moment of deep contemplation, she responded.

"They are bigger, stronger and faster than you. Don't try to overpower them. If you do, they will tear you to pieces. Avoid their strikes at all costs. The only way to beat them is to outsmart and out-maneuver them. But the truth is… this battle is going to be a longshot."

Her words trailed off. On the outside she seemed calm and focused, but Roki could tell from the look in her eye that she was worried. He could see her doubt. She didn't think that they would survive it.

Chapter XIII

Roki stared awestruck at the large group of orcs as they began closing the last three hundred feet. He could see their shapes in much better detail. They were tall, a few of the largest being close to eight feet. Their grey skin was thin, with a hint of blue color. Large angular muscles bulged from their bare, scar-covered chests and arms, while thick, black fur covered their lower bodies. They ran upright on two feet like most common races, but their odd posture seemed to have more in common with a wild beast. Their large, powerful legs carried their heavy upper bodies with ease. Most of the raging orcs held crude clubs or gnarled maces in their hands as they charged.

Leena was right, they were strong and fast. How could the three of them stand against an army of superior enemies? He flinched in reflex as the loud sound began thundering from Leena's bow. *THWAP, THWAP, THWAP, THWAP, THWAP*. She fired arrow after arrow in rapid succession towards the large group. For every two or three arrows, Roki could see one of the heavy beasts go down. It was working, but not fast enough. There was no way she would take out enough of them in time. If it was over, he wasn't going out without a fight. His grip clenched down hard on the warm handle of his hammer as he anticipated the imminent attack. His heart pounded in his chest. *THOOM, THOOM, THOOM*. He struggled to take a deep, nervous breath. The orcs were almost to them. One hundred feet. Ninety feet. Eighty. He could feel the muscles in his arms tightening up. They felt strong. It was good. He would need every bit of strength he could get.

As the group barreled towards them, he took one last glance at his friends. Leena had moved in close to his right shoulder, still firing arrows rapidly. Dax had drawn in to his left and stood ready to defend their position. It looked like they were all on their own.

Roki bent his knees and readied his strike. He braced for the impact. The group of orcs slammed into the heroes with a loud clash of steel and iron. He jumped to the side as the first few orcs charged directly at him. He rolled across the soft ground and quickly jumped back to his feet. He didn't wait for the first attack. He wound up hard and released, sending the sparkling steel maul slamming into the midsection of a lunging orc. The impact was surprisingly more forceful than he had anticipated. The large heavy creature was sent instantly rolling backwards into the oncoming attackers, tripping them as they charged. Roki wasted no time waiting for them to recover. He sent another strong swing hurling and spun around to meet the others that now surrounded him. The maul collided with another creature's torso with a loud crack as the beast tumbled off to the side

He didn't have much time to think about his friends as more orcs reached him. One of the large orcs jumped ahead of the group and brought his giant club up high into the air. It brought the club down hard with a roar as it lunged at Roki. The big wooden club dropped down right above his head, but he moved to the side just in time as the club slammed into the ground with a thud. The orc wasted no time and lashed out sideways for a second attack. Roki jumped back a foot or two to narrowly miss the impact. The orc's evaded swing whizzed through the air and collided with another orcs face with a crunching sound. He looked back just in time to duck under another orc's attack. The failure of impact sent the orc off balance. Roki took advantage of the opportunity and slammed the heavy maul into the orc's chest. The steel impacted with a loud noise as it crushed the bones beneath and knocked it back.

Roki turned back quickly towards the other orcs just as another club barreled towards his head. He ducked low as he took a few steps to the side and swung. The heavy maul struck the beast hard in the side, causing it to let out a loud roar. He followed up with another strike to the orc's head, sending it toppling over. He looked back. Another orc charged at him with its arms high above its head, gripping its heavy club. As the creature moved towards him, Roki jumped forward and kicked his foot hard against the creature's lower midsection. The impact wasn't what he expected. His kick slammed into the orc like it was hitting a stone wall. Pain shot through his foot as the impact sent him backwards a few feet. It hadn't even slowed the orc's advance.

The large creature brought its club down hard with a loud snarl. Roki rolled across the ground just in time to barely dodge the hit. The club crashed hard into the ground next to him. Roki jumped to his feet and went for the only attack he had time for. He gripped his weapon in an underhand position and brought it up with all his speed and strength. The heavy maul slammed into the orc's chin with a bang, exploding the bottom half of the creature's head.

He only had a split second to canvass the area before the next group of orcs closed in. He looked over at Leena who battled fiercely a few feet away. Her agility and speed where no match for the overly-large mob that surrounded her. She needed help. All at once Roki leaned forward and charged. As he reached her position he reared back and pulled hard on the heavy hammer, slamming it into two or three of the attacking orcs.

The attack knocked two of the creatures back into another group, lessening her burden for a moment. Roki turned around to meet another forceful attack. He brought his hammer up just in time to block the brunt of the force as the heavy mace slammed into him. The force sent him spinning off into the ground. He rolled quickly back onto his feet to brace for the follow up attack. As the large orc moved in, an arrow slammed into the side of its neck, causing it to let out a painful-sounding squeal. Roki jumped forward and struck the side of its head hard with his hammer, dropping it instantly. Before he could turn around to look for the next attack something slammed into his left shoulder.

The impact of the wooden club slamming into him sent his body flying a few feet. Pain tore through his arm as he landed on the ground. There was no time to coddle his injury before the next attack came crashing down towards his face. He rolled with a loud grunt, barely missing the brutal collision as the weapon struck the ground. He staggered onto his feet and ducked a heavy iron battle axe as it sliced through the air above his head. He grabbed on tight to the hard steel handle of his hammer and let loose a powerful but wild swing in the direction of the incoming orcs.

The hammer collided with one of the orcs on the left and sent its heavy body slamming into the others. He brought the hammer down hard on top of one of the fallen orc's head. The strong bone crushed beneath the heavy steel maul like a clay pot. Roki quickly let loose another swing before turning around to avoid the next attack. A particularly heavy looking orc charged at him, holding a giant steel maul above its head. As it reached him, it let out a furious battle cry and lunged. There was no way he could fight against the creature with brute strength alone. If it landed the attack, he would be finished. He would have to take Leena's advice and out-maneuver it.

Roki jumped to the side at the last second as the giant maul came roaring down towards him. In the same motion brought his hammer down at an angle into the orc's knee. The bones buckled easily beneath the steel hammer, causing the orc to let out a furious growl. It swung its large arm back up quickly, slamming into Roki's chest. The impact pushed him up into the air and back, knocking the breath out of him. He landed a few feet away and immediately fell into a kneeling position. He struggled to breath. Just then he heard Leena's voice cry out in pain. He looked up just in time to see her fly backwards. She was surrounded.

He glanced over at Dax who was still fighting violently. Dax wouldn't be able to get to her in time.

He had to do something. Shaking off the last attack, Roki charged forwards towards the horde. Sidestepping another strike, he swung into an orc's body as he spun around. He didn't let the motion slow him down. He pushed forward with everything. Just before he reached the orcs, he drew up the heavy hammer with both arms and brought it down hard, hurling it forward with every bit of his strength.

Strong pains tore through his injured arm as the heavy weapon left his hands. The weapon soared through the air and crashed into the orc directly in front of him, throwing it forward violently. The impact didn't seem to slow the hammer's movement as it continued forward into a large group, knocking them back several feet.

Roki didn't waste a second. He ran to where the hammer had dropped and grasped onto the handle again. With all his speed and strength, he swung it up and out, crushing the bones of the next orc's face. The force sent the creature flipping backwards in to the recovering pile of orcs. Leena was already to her feet, with a thin, steady stream of red blood pouring down from the left side of her head and onto her cheek.

Seeing her injury made him furious. But before he could enact his revenge, a heavy object collided with his upper back, pushing him forward. He dropped to the ground and let out a loud scream as the searing pain shot through his body. Time around him seemed to slow down as he writhed in agony. It felt like his shoulder blade had been shattered. He had to get up. They would be on top of him at any second.

His heart pounded as the ugly orc quickly closed in towards him, ready to finish the job. He had to do something. He tried to bring his weapon up, but the pressure caused even more agonizing pain. Just as the creature reached him, several arrows slammed into its chest from the side. The arrows pierced cleanly through its ribcage and out the other side, dropping the heavy orc to the ground instantly. More arrows whizzed past him and slammed into the horde.

Roki staggered to his feet as the next wave hit. Leena quickly dodged a few attacks and fired another precise arrow, dropping her attacker like a stone block. Roki turned around just in time to see an orc lunge at him. It swung its heavy weapon hard. He tried to pull up on the steel hammer, but it was difficult. The weight pulled on his painful injury. He took in a quick deep breath and sidestepped the wild club attack, bringing the hammer up into the orcs ribcage. The creature let out a painful snarl and swung its club again.

This time he couldn't clear its wide swing. The collision barely caught his left shoulder again, sending him flying sideways. The reactivated pain in his left shoulder rang out again. Being injured on both sides of his body was pure torture. He stumbled a few feet and fell to his knees. The large creatures were just too strong. There were too many.

As he hopelessly planned out his next move, the next wave of attackers closed in. There was no time. He was surrounded. This was it. As the next orc lunged, something caught him off guard. Dax charged in towards him and jumped in front of the orc's attack, bringing his shiny sword up to block the blow, with his round shield simultaneously deflecting a few strikes from the side. As the orc's iron sword struck Dax's shiny silver blade, a blinding flash of light shot out. The bright red light forced Roki's eyes to shut as he turned his head away. As the daze of the flash subsided he cracked open his eyes and looked up.

He was still disoriented but he could see silhouettes of the large orcs staggering backwards. After a second his eyes refocused and he could see the group of orcs in front of him staggering back and forth grabbing their eyes. They seemed to have been temporarily blinded by the light of Dax's sword.

Dax and Leena wasted no time and rushed in to attack the unsuspecting orcs. Hard slashes of Dax's sharp sword and a flurry of arrows from Leena's bow brought a good number of the creatures down fast. Roki put his left hand on his knee and pushed himself up. Despite the pain, he had to help while they had the upper hand. He gritted his teeth through the pain and charged forward.

Gripping the hammer tightly he swung into another small group. The hammer slammed into them hard, dropping all but two. He quickly spun around and planted another attack into a creature's lower spine, crushing it in. The orc let out a painful shriek as it dropped. A forceful strike to the last orc's head sent it sailing off. Roki dropped the heavy hammer to the ground and breathed in deep.

He looked out over the battlefield. The number of orcs was dwindling by the second. Within a minute or two they would all be gone. He looked at the random orc bodies that littered the ground for nearly two hundred feet in front of him. They had done it. They had survived the orcs, but just barely.

As Dax and Leena moved to finish off the last few orcs, Roki closed in to lend a hand. A heavy swing from his hammer sent two orcs flying while two or three arrows from Leena's bow finished the rest. As the last orc hit the ground, Roki came to a stop in front of his two friends. They were breathing almost as heavy as he was. He took in a few deeper breaths and tried to calm his racing heart. They all stood silent for a moment as they looked around at their conquered foes. It was hard to believe.

He looked back at Leena, whose long dark hair swirled around and rested on her leather clad shoulders. Her body was a little slimmer than usual, probably from all the recent fighting and lack of food.

She held her bow in her left arm and one of her daggers in her right. Her stance was strong and agile looking. Her dark clothing was torn open here and there, exposing a few deep cuts. The expression on her face was serious and focused. Dax looked to be in fair condition, aside from a couple large nasty bruises across the right side of his face from where a club must have struck. A few thin streams of blood ran down from the corner of his right eye over a swollen cheek bone. Another stream of red blood poured from a deep gash across his upper left arm. As the group huddled up, Dax's voice broke the silence.

"Is everyone okay?" Dax asked, out of breath.

Silence ensued for a few moments as the three of them tried to relax their nerves.

"I'm okay," Leena answered as she placed her fingers over her bloodied head wound.

Roki looked down over his own body and then back at Dax. "I've been better, but I will survive," he answered.

Dax gave a quick nod to them and then turned around and walked a few feet away from the orc bodies. He and Leena followed and the three of them stood staring into the dark trees far ahead.

"This is it, guys," Dax spoke.

"Inside that forest ahead is where our journey ends."

After a quick pause he added, "Whatever waits for us in there, we face it together. Agreed?"

Roki returned an accepting nod.

"Agreed," Leena said firmly.

As they moved towards the dark tree line, Roki looked out over the decimated battlefield one final time. They had barely escaped the last battle with their lives. They had gotten lucky. He didn't know what was waiting for them deep inside the heart of the forest, but he wasn't so sure they were ready to face it. They would soon find out, one way or another.

Chapter XIV

Being back inside the forest felt much safer, even if it was dark and eerie. Leena liked the feeling of being surrounded by trees and plants, regardless of the threat of danger that might lurk inside. She had nearly spent more of her life inside a forest than she had outside of it. It felt natural to her. She didn't particularly like the new area though. It had a strangely benevolent atmosphere about it. It was hard to put a finger on exactly what was wrong with it, but she knew it didn't feel natural.

She walked along cautiously as they advanced in their normal formation, her body weak and rigid. All she could think about was being back in her soft bed, but she knew it would be some time before she got to rest again. They still had to face the obstacles ahead of them. She needed to stay strong and focused.

Leena followed behind Dax for nearly an hour as he pushed ahead through the heavy brush and twisted tree limbs. Occasionally a razor-sharp thorn would catch her just right and slice open a small cut across her arm or thigh. It didn't take long for her to accumulate a myriad of small cuts across both sides of her body. The small cuts were more annoying than painful.

As they walked, the forest seemed to grow more alive than the previous parts. Long thick vines dropped from the forest ceiling and deep green-colored plants grew all up and down the tree trunks, with a thick moss blanketing the forest floor. But something also felt off about it. It was warmer than it should've been, and quite humid. The grass and trees were damp with moisture, almost as if they perspired in the heat. It seemed to get warmer the deeper they went. The entire area gave her a bad feeling.

Leena's attention turned to Roki, who was pacing only a foot or two behind. He was closer to her than normal. Maybe he was scared. Maybe he was trying to use her as a shield to guard his injuries. Or maybe he wanted to protect her. She didn't know which it was, but she didn't mind it, if it helped to relax him. Dax paced silently, a few feet off to their left. The pinkish-red glow from his sword provided them enough light to see, though there were still a fair number of shadowy crevices and blind spots ahead.

More time passed by as they pushed deeper and deeper into the living sauna. The temperature had increased considerably, to the point that the air was thick and wet. It stuck to her lungs and made it hard to breath. Struggling to catch a good breath made her body even more fatigued. She continued forward with her finger tips perched on her bowstring, ready to fire at a second's notice. There was no way to know what might by watching them, waiting for a chance to strike.

Large plant-covered stones and downed tree trunks littering the ground made it difficult to keep her attention on her surroundings. She tried to keep her eyes on the shadowy trees ahead as she scaled over large, moss-covered stones and ducked under low-hanging limbs, having to force herself to slow down every so often to give the other two a chance to catch up. They didn't move as easily through the dense forest as she did.

A bead of sweat rolled down her right brow and onto her cheek bone as she ducked under the next branch. It was getting hotter. She could feel a faint migraine starting to form in the back of her head from her prior injury. Her chest felt heavy as she forced in a breath of the invisible mist.

Leena moved through the hot forest hoping for even the smallest breeze to penetrate the heavy barrier. As she pushed through the next patch of overgrown weeds and branches, she immediately dropped down into a crouching position and stopped. She held up her hand, signaling the Dax and Roki to stop behind her. The sound of their heavy boots came to a halt a few feet back.

She looked out over the area in front of her. The thick trees and brush rolled away into a large clearing, with a nearly impenetrable line of trees enclosing the entire area like a wall. On the ground in front of her rested a mostly overgrown path, made of smooth, grey stone. The path extended for nearly a hundred feet ahead before ending at the base of a large stone structure that appeared to be some king of long abandoned temple ruins. The cracked and rugged stone walls rose straight up into the forest ceiling and disappeared into the darkness above. Large granite pillars sat on either side of the huge stone ruins, decorated with ornate symbols.

There were no signs of life, but the structure seemed to have a presence of its own. The area around the large doorway was littered with chunks of shattered, dull-grey stone that seemed to have made up a barrier at one time but now lay in rubble, revealing the pitch-black darkness inside. A snapping twig next to her let her know that her friends had closed in for a better look.

After scanning the area for a moment, she glanced over at Dax for the confirmation. He looked over the area himself before readying his sword and moving ahead to take the lead. Leena followed close behind, ready for anything. As they inched towards the towering stone ruins, she could immediately start to feel the cool air flowing out from the dark doorway. Its cave-like temperature immediately rushed across her sweaty scalp and forehead, cooling her body down. It felt strangely inviting.

She inched forward towards the doorway, being cautious of what might wait inside. After moving up a small set of stone stairs, they advanced into the dark corridor. Her vision was better than theirs, but it was still hard to see. As Dax held his sword up high, the bright light poured forth into the room. They were standing in some kind of entrance chamber. To their left and right, large staircases curved around and disappeared upwards, probably leading to some long-abandoned bell tower.

In front of them, the room opened up into a larger area with an ancient-looking assortment of heavy jars and stone basins lining the room. At the far end, the floor gave way to a stone staircase that led down into the darkness below. They moved forward toward the opposite end of the room with caution, careful to avoid stepping on the random pieces of metal and worthless artifacts strewn across the dusty stone floor. They navigated silently through the room and over to the staircase. Leena looked down into the dark silence below, trying not to imagine what horror might be waiting for them. After a few seconds of studying the shadows, Dax motioned for them to follow as he began to walk slowly down the stone steps.

She couldn't help but feel uneasy as the three of them descended into the unknown below. At the bottom of the stairs, a rush of cold whipped across her face. It was even colder than the room above. The previously warm beads of sweat now sent shivers down her spine as the cold air rushed around her neck. As the light from Dax's sword illuminated the area, she immediately started to scan the room for danger.

After a few seconds, Leena lowered her bowstring and looked around. They were standing in a long, narrow room with a high ceiling. Giant cob-web covered chandeliers hung motionless high above them. Thick dusty chains used for lowering the chandeliers dropped down to iron posts on the sides of the wall to the left. In between the three chains rested two dark passages. On the opposite side of the room two more passages mirrored the others. As they moved quietly across the room, she paid close attention to the side passages, anticipating a surprise attack. Her mind eased up slightly as she looked at the thick layer of dust across the stone floor. It didn't appear as though anything had come through the room in quite some time.

She felt her nerves relax a bit as she looked to the doorway ahead. Everything seemed undisturbed. She continued to follow Dax as they quickly made their way through the doorway and into the next dark corridor. The corridor was narrow and long, the light from Dax's sword reflecting off the grey stone floor just well enough to allow them to see ahead. As they moved forward, Leena could see Dax's hand tighten on the handle of his sword as he held his round shield up high near his chest, in an overly cautious position. She could see the anxiety in his hands as he inched into the darkness ahead, ready to attack.

As she advanced, she waited for some sign of movement or sound, but there wasn't any. It was quiet and still, aside from the faint whipping echo of the cold air as it moved. The long dark corridor stretched for what seemed like a few hundred feet before ending abruptly at another downward set of stairs. She could feel a small amount worry started to creep up into her throat as she moved down the smooth, cold, stone steps. Something about the place didn't feel right. Why was it so quiet? Why hadn't any animals taken shelter inside?

After a short hallway they came into a small square room with only a single doorway leading out. The room was filled with barrels, chests, and wooden racks full of dusty weapons and armor. After a quick glance around, Dax and Roki immediately began rummaging through the equipment in search of anything valuable. Leena watched the room as they worked.

After she was sure that there wasn't any immediate danger, she turned towards the others. Roki inspected a heavy-looking steel cuirass while Dax gripped a fine steel shield in his left hand. Her view drifted over to a wooden jar off in the corner. The long feather fletching stuck up from a bundle of arrows. She hadn't depleted her stock of arrows yet, but it wouldn't hurt to replenish her quiver, just in case. She moved through the crates and stands over to where the arrows rested and grabbed a large handful.

They were made well and still in good condition. The silver tips still looked razor-sharp. She reached back and stuffed them into her quiver until it was nearly full and then began to look around some more. In a small wooden chest next to her she spotted a pile of various gemstones. She quickly shoved a few into her pocket as something else caught her eye. Behind the chest, draped over a wooden armor stand, was a beautiful set of golden ring mail armor. It would be perfect to go over her leather. It was light and maneuverable, but yet its reinforced metal would protect her from being sliced open.

She quickly looked around and then, without hesitation, dropped her bow and quiver to the ground silently. She grabbed the nearly weightless ring mail armor and slipped it over her head. It felt nice and light as it fell on to her body. It was a good fit. She quickly picked up her quiver and strapped it back over her shoulder as she grabbed up her bow into her hand. Roki and Dax had also started suiting themselves up. Roki grabbed the heavy pieces of steel armor from the stand in front of him while Dax went for the much lighter set of scale mail in the corner.

After a few moments they had finished and were ready. Leena moved toward the doorway and let Dax advance. She readied an arrow and followed close behind. Their movements now echoed into the dark hallway as Roki's heavy steel armor clanked with each step. Dax held the new steel shield out in front of him. It was long and came to a point at the bottom, dropping down close to his knees. He held his sword out in front to light the way.

They passed through several more dark and empty rooms before soon coming across another descending staircase. As they reached the bottom of the stairs, she was struck with a rush of hot humid air that immediately felt heavy in her lungs. It was odd to feel such a warm breeze inside of the cool stone structure. She looked around the area curiously. They were standing in a large room. The stone walls and ceiling extended quite a way ahead of them before giving way to thick vines and trees trunks. At some point a cave-in had allowed the forest to grow into the ruins.

At the opposite end of the room, the dark foliage nearly erased any evidence of the stone structure. As she looked around the area, she noticed a narrow passage where a doorway must have once been. She nodded her head to let the others know. The three of them moved over to the small passage and peered inside. The light of Dax's sword did little to illuminate the area beyond. Slowly, they pushed through the small opening into the next area. It opened up into a large space. The crumbled stone floor was nearly all that remained of the massive structure that once stood there. The ceiling was completely gone, and the thick treetops above nearly blocked out any trace of sunlight. Large, dark tree trunks grew in from both sides, nearly consuming what was left of the crumbling stone walls.

As they advanced through the dense trees and vines Leena kept her bowstring pulled tight. Something was off about the place, and it seemed to bother her more and more with every step. They passed over the rubble and through a space between two large tree trunks. She ducked a few low-hanging branches and vines and moved ahead. As soon as they were past the thickest area, the forest receded back out again, revealing more of the stone ruins ahead.

She moved forward with caution. The stone walls rose up high again off to the sides as she passed under a chunk of the stone ceiling. Soon she was back inside of the stone ruins again. They advanced slowly through another dark corridor and rounded a corner. They came to an abrupt stop just inside the next room.

It was a very big circular room with a dozen or so stone crypts lining the walls. In the center of the room, stone steps dropped down to a large flat area. In the middle rested a stone altar. Golden inscriptions were carved into the floor around the altar in a wide circle. It looked to be some kind of ancient burial chamber. She had never seen anything like it. Something very odd caught her eye. Lined around the room, attached firmly to the stone walls, were six dimly glowing torches. The flames were an odd blue color, exactly like the strange flames that they had encountered earlier in the forest. The sight of them caused a nervous pain in the pit of her stomach. Someone, or something, had to have lit the torches at some point. What if they were still there?

Chapter XV

Dax motioned for her and Roki to follow as he advanced towards the stone altar at the center of the room. Leena followed close behind with an arrow ready. She tried not to let the blue flames distract her as she scanned the room, taking special care to inspect the shadowy corners. As Dax moved cautiously towards the strange altar, suddenly the dim, blue flames exploded outwards from the torches, forming into a bright inferno at the center of the room in front of them. The blue flames swirled violently around in the air before splitting into four parts. The small beams of fire shot out to the sides of the room and fell down like silk, passing right through the heavy stone lids that rested atop the burial crypts.

It became instantly dark as the blue flames disappeared into the large stone crypts. The soft pinkish-red glow of Dax's blade slowly brightened the area, growing in intensity until Leena could see her surroundings clearly once again. She waited silently, baffled by the strange occurrence. Suddenly she heard a loud thud coming from the far edges of the room to her left, then another. The floor beneath her feet began to shake as the noise continued to quicken. All at once the five crypts burst outwards, shattering the heavy stone into pieces. She jumped back, struggling to see, as a large cloud of dust rolled forth.

As the dust started to settle, Leena glanced around the room at the spots where the crypts had been. Her eyes grew wide at the discovery. Slowly rising to their feet were four ominous-looking skeletons, the eye-sockets of their gnarled skulls burning bright with the treacherous blue flames. Their bodies were large and covered in ornate silver armor and they each gripped a giant steel claymore in their hands.

The dusty metal scraped over the stone floor as they dragged the weapons, starting towards them. Their movements seemed jerky and unnatural, as if they were mere puppets on a string. Leena's mind raced as the undead minions walked towards her. What kind of magic was this? How would they be able to fight against it?

She had to try something. She pulled back on the sturdy bow and fired, sending an arrow barreling towards one of their heads. The arrow struck the creature's hard skull and ricocheted off into the dark. She dismissed it with a scowl and quickly fired another. The arrow slammed into the glowing blue eye socket of another skeleton and disintegrated with a flash. Before she could fire again, Roki charged in and swung his heavy steel hammer.

The attack slammed into the chest plate of the undead skeleton, sending it flying backwards into the hard wall. It dropped to the ground like a heavy stone. Her relief soon wore off as the fallen minion slowly rose back to its feet and continued its advance. What were they going to do? How could they stop enemies that weren't even alive?

The fear rose up into her throat as the grim creatures pushed forward. Suddenly Dax charged in and slammed into the three in front with his large shield. The impact barely sent them back a few feet. It didn't seem to affect their persistence one bit. Dax followed up with a big swing with his sharp sword. The blade bounced off the skeleton's hard skull with a spark. Another strike produced the same results.

One of the skeletons swung its giant sword at Dax's head, missing by an inch. As Dax ducked backwards, Roki charged in again and let loose a massive swing. The hammer collided with the side of the hostile creature, sending it flying into the others. As they stumbled backwards she decided to capitalize on the opportunity by letting loose a barrage of arrows.

Shot after shot the sharp arrows ricocheted off in random directions as they slammed into the hard bone. Dax and Roki took the opportunity to fall back towards her and regroup.

"What are we going to do?" Roki stuttered frantically.

"I don't know," Dax responded. "We can't seem to hurt them, not this way at least."

Leena looked over the room quickly and then back at the marching skeletons. They didn't seem too fast. It gave her an idea.

"We can't just stand here," she said quickly. "Maybe we can fan out and let them chase us for a bit until we can come up with a plan."

Dax and Roki both agreed and moved away in separate directions. It wasn't going to keep them alive forever, but maybe it would buy them enough time to figure out a way to defeat their enemies.

One of the vile minions turned towards her as she backed away in the other direction. Leena moved quickly along the edge of the room trying to think about a possible strategy. What could they do? She fired a few more arrows at the skeleton with some ill-fated hope that it would do some harm. The arrows pinged off into the darkness just as the others had. Her attacks only seemed to motivate the creature to move ahead more aggressively.

It leaned forward and swung hard with its heavy sword. The rusty blade buzzed past her face as she leaped backwards. It didn't slow down. Its hollow, flaming, blue eye-sockets seemed to burn brighter as it lunged forward again with another massive swing. Once more, she swiftly evaded the attack. The tactic wasn't going to work for long. The room was only so big, and it was just a matter of time before they would run into each other. If the menacing skeletons managed to corner them somehow, it could mean dire consequences.

A quick glance back at Dax and Roki let her know that the other minions were growing more aggressive as well. They had to figure out something fast. Her attacker seemed to understand her sense of desperation as it jumped forward again, swinging wildly. The edge of the blade barely caught her upper arm, causing a quick sharp pain where the metal sliced into her flesh. She let out a feminine grunt and moved back quickly. How was she going to stop this thing? Her bow was no use against it. Using her daggers would place her entirely too close to the creature.

The familiar steel of Roki's large hammer slammed into her attacker's body, sending it hurling off into the stone wall. Roki must've heard her cry and come to help. She turned and looked as Roki lunged back towards his own stalkers and landed a massive blow, knocking them backwards a dozen feet. As the two skeletons landed on the stone floor, the impact jarred one of their helmets loose, sending it pinging across the hard stone. Seeing the bare, round skull of the menacing creature gave her an idea. Maybe with a strong enough blow, Roki's hammer would be heavy enough to crush the hard bone.

"Roki!" she cried out. "Go for its head!" But it was too late. The gnarled skeleton corpse had already begun to stand up. Its skull would need to be against the ground to produce the right amount of force. She looked up just in time to dodge another swing. As the next swing came towards her she ducked low and spun her body around quickly. At the last second, she kicked out her left leg, sweeping the armor-clad minion off of its feet. In the same motion she slammed her hands into the creature's body, sending it tumbling backwards. It would buy her just enough time to do what she needed to. She charged forward in Roki's direction. As she reached the helmetless skeleton, she jumped forward, evading another attack, and brought her bow limb up behind its knees. The blow knocked the creature into the air as she brought her bow back around on top of its chest, slamming it into the ground.

"Now, Roki!" she barked.

Roki turned just as his last strike connected with one of the foul creatures. He drew up his heavy steel hammer and charged viciously ahead. Just before he reached her, he threw the weight of his weapon up into the air and pushed his boots against the stone floor. The leap sent him up into the air directly above the skeleton. As his body descended, he swung down furiously, letting out a loud grunt.

The steel maul flashed in front of her face as it barreled towards the corpse's dense skull. A wave of blue light shot out like an explosion as the hammer connected with a gigantic crash. The force of the blue energy immediately threw her and Roki back a dozen feet like a sack of cotton. She slammed into the wall behind her with a grunt as it knocked the breath out of her lungs. Her eyes crossed as the dizziness from the impact set in.

Through drifting sets of images, she could make out Roki slumped against a wall not far away from her. As the images began to converge, she couldn't believe what she was seeing. The skeleton was rising to its feet, unscathed. It's exposed skull still glowing faintly all around with the blue light. What manner of magic was this? She didn't understand. The massive attack should've turned its skull to powder. It was like the creatures were completely immune to physical harm.

There was no way to stop them. Fear began to set in as the malefic corpses marched towards her. There was no point in running. She was completely surrounded. She had no way to stop the dark magic. How could they have been so foolish to think that they had a chance against it? Her body trembled as the foul minion drew up its heavy blade, ready to deliver the fatal blow. The dreadful blue flames surged inside of its hollow eyes. Her mind flashed with memories and emotions as she accepted her gruesome fate. With a jerk the ominous corpse swung its weapon down towards her head. She closed her eyes tight, anticipating the painful strike.

Suddenly, a loud clash of steel caused her to jump. Leena opened her eyes just in time to see a brilliant red beam of light flash in front of her face as the dark corpse's head dropped to the floor. Its hulking body soon followed. No sooner than its body touched the ground the foul creature burst into a roaring blue flame. She shielded her eyes from the bright blue light and looked up at the familiar shape of her friend. Dax was standing over her, holding his sword tightly in his hand, the blade pulsing brightly as brilliant red flames flowed up the length of the steel. He stood breathing heavily, staring down at the burning corpse. The light from the blue flames burned brightly, illuminating his vengeful expression. Within a matter of seconds, the flame was gone, and with it the fallen corpse.

Leena glanced over as the three remaining creatures closed in. Their motions seemed angry as they drew their weapons up high and charged towards him. She wanted to help him, but her weapon had already proved to be useless against the dark magic. She could only look on in fear. The disgusted look on Dax's face grew more obvious as he turned towards the other skeletons. He drew his glowing sword up high and let out a furious battle cry.

As the first foe reached him, he sidestepped its violent attack and unleashed a wild slash, slicing clean though its torso. The two halves dropped to the ground like heavy boulders. He spun around, ready for the next attack. Ducking swiftly under the swing, he brought the red blade up hard into the corpse's arms, severing them instantly at the elbow joint. Then he brought the sword around and down again quickly, slicing through its helmet-covered skull. As the large chunk of bone flew away, more blue fire burst upwards towards the ceiling.

The final creature's attack came a split-second before Dax could ready his shield. The edge of the steel blade slid across the right side of his head, opening up a deep gash. The blow sent him stumbling backwards. As Dax struggled to recover, she could see the red blood pour down his face and onto the floor. He looked dazed. The creature moved to strike again just as Roki's hammer collided with its chest plate. It stumbled backwards a couple of feet and moved in again.

Roki locked weapons with it, as it brought down another heavy attack. The force seemed to nearly buckle Roki at the knees, but he managed to hold it back. Leena could see the strain on his face as he struggled to push against the skeleton corpse's unnatural strength. Slowly the large sword inched down towards Roki's head. He wouldn't be able to hold it off for long. She looked at Dax who was desperately trying to wipe the blood from his eye long enough to see. There wasn't time, she had to help.

Leena staggered to her feet and charged forward. As she reached the skeleton, she slammed into its side with her shoulder, giving Roki just enough advantage to land a short blow to its back, sending it spinning off towards the wall. Just as Roki went for another strike, Dax swooped in and let loose a furious swing. The searing red flame sliced easily through the skeleton's armor clad upper torso, dropping it to the ground. Leena stood by, awestruck, as the last enemy corpse dropped and burst into a roaring blue flame.

She stared with glazed-over eyes as the bright flames swirled aggressively around the body. After a few seconds they were standing alone once again in the dark burial room. It would have been completely dark if not for the magical red fire of Dax's sword. She and Roki walked slowly over to Dax and gazed upon the mesmerizing red glow emanating from his sword. It was magnificent. The bright red flame swirled and weaved as it moved up and down the shiny blade, pulsing with energy.

"How...?" Roki's voice trailed off.
"It must be the fairy enchantment," Dax said, as he stared into the red flame.

"I saw the undead creature lunge at Leena and I reacted without thinking. I swung the sword violently, hoping for a miracle. The blade seemed to react somehow to my desperation."

With Dax's words, Leena thought over everything that had happened. In all the chaos of battle she had forgotten about the fairy's enchantments. She stared down at her own weapon. Why hadn't her bow shown any properties of the enchantments? Roki's hammer hadn't displayed any signs of power either. Were they filled with some other type of magic, she wondered? Her heart fluttered nervously as a low, chilling sound echoed through the room.

"Sooo you defeated my minionsss did you?" the voice rasped.

Leena looked around the room, trying to track down the source. There was no one in the room besides the three of them.

"Where is that coming from?" Dax whispered over his shoulder as he darted his head around.

Again, the dark voice echoed through the room.

"Do you really thinkk you can ssstand against me? I will rend on your bones!" the voice roared.

Leena started to get a bad feeling in the pit of her stomach as she scanned the dark room. Where was the menacing voice coming from? She started to think that they had made a terrible mistake. Suddenly the hidden foe let out a terrifying laugh. As the wicked laugh echoed through the room, a fearful chill ran down her spine as the tiny hairs on the back of her neck stood up. She could feel her hands trembling against her long wooden bow. She didn't know what was about to happen, but she didn't want to stick around and find out. It wasn't worth their lives.

"We have to get out of here," she whispered frantically.

Dax turned his head back quickly and looked at her.

"Do you really think this creature is going to let us leave this place alive?" he answered.

Leena scowled unintentionally as she thought over his words. Her heart sank a little more. He was right. There was no escape. Deep down she knew that it wouldn't let them leave. They had to face it. But how? Dax's sword seemed to now possess a great power, but she and Roki were completely defenseless against the dark magic. She was a good warrior when fighting against flesh and steel, but this was beyond her skills.

Suddenly the ground started to rumble as the wall across from her began to shake, sliding aside to reveal a hidden passage leading to another dark room. She could barely see a faint blue glow radiating deep inside. She looked at Dax and Roki, who looked back with the same expression. It was going to end, one way or the other.

Chapter XVI

Leena and the others made their way across the room and into the corridor. The eerie blue light resonated from a short way ahead. She ducked low as the ceiling dropped down in front of her, narrowing the passage. A short d further and the passage opened back up into a large dark chamber. Part of the room had collapsed in several spots, allowing the overgrown forest foliage to grow in. In the center of the room a massive black tree grew up out of the ground, pushing aside the grey stone floor. It rose straight up for nearly thirty feet before branching off and disappearing into the dark unknown heights above. At the base of the large tree rested a shallow looking pool of black water.

As Leena's eyes finished instinctively scanning the lines of the room, her attention drifted back towards the source of the soft blue light. Two glowing spheres of flame hovered among the shadows near the large tree trunk. Terror gripped her as the blue spheres drifted forwards, revealing their true host. There, towering in the shadows, stood a dreadful and terrifying looking figure. Rotting and mangled flesh hung from its fresh-looking corpse. Covering its decaying body was the most devious looking black armor imaginable, the edge of each piece sharpened like razors. Covering its wicked looking skull was a king's battle crown. The battle crown had long, steel face guards extending down to the creature's chin, and the top was socketed with precious-looking stones.

The overly-large, undead corpse stood in place with his head slanted in an unnatural looking position, his half-decayed eyes glowing brightly with the strange blue fire. Leena jumped back with anticipation as the lurking zombie dropped its mangled jaw to speak.

"Welcome to my burialll chamberrr..," the zombie rasped.

As its jaw moved up and down, dark black liquid dripped from its mouth and onto the ground. The gruesome sight made her stomach turn.

"Soon it will be yoursss assss welll..," it spoke.

Leena pulled back on the loaded arrow in anticipation. She could feel her arms shaking with fatigue from her injuries, mixed with her fear of the towering darkness.

She watched as Dax stepped forward. "What do you want?" Dax rattled off, in a shaky voice. With Dax's words the towering zombie let out a baneful laugh. Its voice echoed around the large room, mocking Dax's question.

"Only your deathhh…" The creature growled, its blue eyes brightening with rage. Leena didn't wait to hear any more of the terrifying banter. She wasn't going to let herself be intimidated any further. She contracted her back muscles forcefully and released her fingers from the thin bow string.

The arrow exploded from the bow and barreled through the air towards the hulking creature. The sharp arrow tore through the weak flesh of the zombie's face easily, splintering as it collided into the hard bone underneath. The zombie let out an annoyed growl and turned towards her. It drew its left arm up high into the air, sending a bright stream of swirling blue light streaking right towards her. Before she could evade the attack, the blue magic slammed into her neck and twisted tightly around her throat, cutting off her air supply.

The vile monster then made an upwards motion with its black, steel-plated gauntlet, lifting her high off of the ground. Leena kicked her feet violently in an effort to get free but it was no use. The creature's dark magic was too strong to fight back against physically. She could feel the weight of her body fighting against her efforts to gain a breath. Dax quickly rushed in towards the giant zombie, the distraction causing the dark creature to release its magic hold on her. The blue magic dissolved instantly, sending her falling to the ground. She landed gracefully on her feet and went down to one knee, gasping for air.

After a rush a cool, stale air entered her lungs, she looked over as Dax drew back with his bright red blade. A blue ball of flame formed in the creature's right hand and quickly shot outward in front of it a short distance, ending with a quick flash. As the flash faded, the undead foe was left holding a long, ethereal sword made of the blue energy. It brought the magical sword up just in time to block Dax's heavy swing.

The two opposing magic blades collided with a flurry of sparks. The tall zombie clearly outmatched Dax's strength as the impact threw Dax's body backwards. Roki wasted no time as he rushed in with his heavy hammer, but before he could get close enough for a strike, the undead foe sent a ball of flame hurling into Roki's chest. The force hit Roki so hard that it lifted him into the air as he flew back like a leaf in the wind. Roki landed on the ground quite a ways back, sliding into the hard stone wall with a thud.

Dax moved back in for another strike. The dark ghoul swung its blue sword hard, slamming into Dax's oncoming attack. The force sent Dax tripping off to the side. Before Dax had even stopped moving, the creature sent a ball of fire slamming into his back.

"No!" Leena cried, as Dax's engulfed body collided with the stone wall, before dropping to the ground. The blue flames faded quickly but Dax wasn't moving. His body was motionless on the ground. The anger exploded inside of her as she screamed and fired a barrage of arrows towards the foul zombie. More blue flames shot up from its left hand, creating a large shield in front of it. The arrows disintegrated immediately as they passed through the flame wall.

It scowled at her with a malicious look and reared back to let loose another attack. Before it could release the ball of fire, a glowing purple object struck hard against its armored body, knocking it backwards. The creature dropped to its knees and slid to a stop. Bright purple bolts of electricity arced all around the foul creature's upper body, somehow seeming to stun its body, at least temporarily.

Leena's eyes drifted back to the bright purple glow. She could hardly believe her eyes. It was Roki. He stood staring at his glowing weapon, his chest moving up and down dramatically as he breathed. His magnificent hammer now possessed a power of its own. Leena looked on in awe at the pulsing purple glow and arcing bolts of electricity as they ran down the surface of the steel maul. The now-recovered creature looked up at Roki and released a flash of energy. The blue light shot outwards in a thin beam, barreling right towards him. Right before it reached Roki, the beam formed into a sharp spike, ripping through the steel armor and flesh of his left shoulder easily. Roki let out a painful scream as the beam of energy lifted him off of the ground by his wound. Roki's agony seemed unbearable as Leena watched his face contort violently. She felt her hands tighten down on her bow handle as the anger of her helplessness grew. In a nearly-blind rage, she quickly let loose a flurry of ill-fated arrows. The thin-shafted projectiles collided with a few strategic positions, but to no effect. The arrows exploded into wooden shards as they impacted the creature's seemingly impenetrable black armor. It didn't seem like her arrows would be of any use against it. But she had to do something.

Just as she was considering rushing in foolishly with her daggers, Dax's form appeared again, battered but alive. He dashed in and swung his red sword at the undead mage-warrior. The red blade released a trail of fire as the zombie brought his blue sword up to deflect the attack. Dax's distraction caused Roki to scream in pain as the blue beam dissolved, releasing him to the ground. Dax fired off several more swings but with the foe's full attention on him, it easily blocked every strike. More blue energy formed in the creature's left hand, quickly producing another sword that mirrored the one in its right hand.

It lunged at Dax, releasing a flurry of strikes. Dax barely moved quickly enough to keep the blades from slicing him in half. But he wouldn't be able to parry the lightning-fast attacks for long. Another spiraling flash of purple light slammed into the creature's chest before it had time to react. The impact released a charge of electricity that arced violently across the zombie's body, causing it to let out a painful roar. The electricity didn't seem to stun the creature nearly as well as the first strike had. Its slower movements seemed only motivate its desire to destroy. The towering creature slammed its armor-clad fist into Roki's chest, sending him flying backwards. Then it leaped forward once again, slashing violently. As the stunning effects of Roki's strike disappeared, Leena could easily notice the drastic increase in the creature's strikes. Dax wouldn't be able to counter them for long. She needed to move in. Before she could move, one of dark zombie's attacks passed through Dax's defenses. The blue blade pierced through Dax's torso easily, exiting out the back. Leena's heart sank in her chest as she looked on, horrified.

"Noooo!" she screamed.

Dax's eyes went wide as the vile creature pulled the blade from his body. Dax's face looked as if he wanted to scream from the pain but wasn't able to. A thin red stream of blood pooled at the corner of his mouth and ran down onto his chin as he dropped to his knees and fell backwards. Roki charged in again, screaming with rage, as he picked up his hammer and began swinging wildly. Leena knew he wouldn't be able to last long.

She felt a tear roll down her cheek as she looked in disbelief at Dax's motionless body. Anger and regret filled her mind. She held on to the smallest hope that he was still alive. She couldn't stand it any longer. She had to do something before the dark creature ended them all. She concentrated hard, trying to think of anything that would save them. It seemed completely hopeless. The creature was too powerful. Its dark magic seemed to flow from an unlimited and unknown source. Even its physical strength far outmatched them. It had no weaknesses. What had they done? For once they were completely outmatched, and their ignorance would cost them everything. She looked over the towering evil being one last time, filled with regret over the foolish mistake. Suddenly something caught her eye. Roki's hammer throw had shattered a small chunk out of the creature's black armor, revealing a pulsing ball of blue light underneath. It pulsed oddly, as if the beating of a heart. Maybe it was a heart. Could it be possible that the dark magic was still bound to the creature in a way that resembled a physical body? She didn't know, but she had to try. It was their only chance. Roki would be gone in a matter of seconds.

Leena closed her eyes and took a deep breath. She concentrated on the power that she knew was inside her weapon. Dax's words ran though her mind about how his weapon had responded to his will. She had to tap into her bow's power or it was all over.

She opened her eyes and focused her aim on the small opening. It would be hard to hit such a small target, especially a moving target. But she had to try. With every ounce of concentration, she released her breath slowly and dropped her fingers from the string. The arrow tore out from the bow with a vengeance, barreling towards the small opening. Leena's eyes widened as she saw the bright green glow of her arrow. She had done it. Her bow had finally released its power. Time seemed to slow to a crawl as she watched the glowing green arrow barrel towards its mark.

Just as it was about to impact, the zombie raised its left arm up high to block it. But its reaction was just slightly too slow, allowing the green-powered arrow to pass just above the creature's forming wall of energy. The bright green arrow whizzed narrowly through the small opening. As soon as it struck the creature's heart, a massive wave of blue light exploded out from inside its body.

The force of the wave threw Roki and Dax into the far wall and sent her rushing back in the opposite direction. The whole room shook violently as the creature screamed in a low agonizing voice. Beams of blue light shot out of its body in multiple directions as it exploded into a raging inferno of blue flame, causing the room to shake even more violently. Leena could feel her body trembling in fear at what might come next. What if her attack had only angered it? After a few moments of violent commotion, the bright blue flame dissipated, leaving nothing left of the creature except a pile of charred armor. She stared ahead, awestruck. She couldn't believe it. The creature was gone. They had defeated it. But she knew it was no time to celebrate.

Leena stared in fear across the room as her two best friends remained motionless. As the rumbling started to fade, she jumped to her feet and rushed over to where her two friends had fallen. As she reached them, Roki awakened from his daze, jerking his body with a gasp. He staggered to his feet, took a few deep breaths and looked around.

"Is it over?" he asked, nervously. She shook her head as she stared back down at Dax's lifeless body.

"I can't believe we won..." he remarked. A well of tears swelled up in her eyes as she realized the cost of their victory.

"No, Roki," she said. "We didn't win anything."
Roki looked down at her, not understanding what she
meant. A mortified look came over his face as he
finally noticed his best friend's body lying on the
ground, not far from his feet. He gripped his left
shoulder in pain as he stared down at Dax's silent
body. The bright red blood had already started to form
a large puddle underneath him. Leena closed her eyes
in heartache as the tears streamed down her cheeks.
Dax was gone.

Suddenly a loud noise rang out high above them as
she felt the ground sway beneath her knees. Leena
looked around the dark room. Another loud noise
followed as a giant chunk of heavy stone fell from the
ceiling far above and slammed into the floor with a
crash. A large crack shot up the wall in front of her as
more chunks of stone shattered across the ground
behind her. The force of the creature's energy
explosion had weakened the structure. It was going to
come down on top of them at any second.

"We have to get out of here!" Roki shouted, as he
looked up into the dark abyss of the high ceiling. "This
whole place is coming down!"

Leena looked back down at her friend's battered
body. "I'm not going to just leave him here!" she cried,
bitterly.

"There's no time, Leena!" Roki shouted back at her.
"He's gone!"

Leena felt more warm tears flow down her face as his words entered her mind. How could she just leave his body behind? Roki knelt down next to her, his own eyes swelling with water. He placed his large hands on her shoulder as he spoke more gently.

"We have to go, Leena."

Roki's words were hard to hear but she knew that he was right. If they didn't move fast they would all be dead. That would mean that Dax's sacrifice meant nothing.

"Okay," she choked, as she wiped the wall of water from her face. She turned around and looked over the room, searching for an exit. The corridor that they had used to enter had collapsed already, blocking their way out. They couldn't go back the way they came. There had to be another way out. Leena glanced around the room frantically, searching for another passage or doorway. There was no other way out. The room they had entered from was the only passage out. They were trapped.

She looked back up at Roki with feelings of regret and despair. The way that Roki looked back at her told her that words were not necessary. He understood. It was too late. It was too late for all of them. Leena leaned in over Dax's still body and cradled his lifeless head in her hands, hugging him tightly. Protecting his body from the gashing stones was the least she could do to honor him. In a few minutes it wouldn't matter anyway. She felt the rush of cold steel against her bare-skinned arm as Roki leaned in over them and wrapped his arms around her. She could feel the warm flow of tears against the back of her neck as he gripped her tightly. At least they would all be together.

Just then Leena heard a loud rumble as a big chunk of the stone ceiling tore off, falling quickly toward them. This was it. She ducked her head against Dax's body and clenched her eyelids tight as the large room started to come down on top of them. Just as the gorge of stone rubble was about to impact, a bright flash of white light flooded the area.

Startled, she opened her eyes curiously, but the blinding brightness didn't allow her to see anything. She could still feel Roki's cold steel armor touching her back. The crashing of the heavy stone ceiling into the ground should have been imminent, but all she could hear was a quiet humming noise. Several seconds passed by and she still could only see the bright white light all around. What was happening? Was she dead?

She looked around at the blissful white glow. Upon closer inspection she could start to see small glowing balls of golden light. The humming also seemed to grow into a more musical sound. Maybe she *was* dead. If so, it was far better than anything she had imagined before. It was quite peaceful. She finally felt safe.

Chapter XVII

Leena's eyes struggled to make out vague shapes as a few colors started to swirl around before her. She watched curiously as they moved to take shape. Soon, familiar figures began to form on every side. She wasn't dead after all. She looked around the beautiful forest sanctuary with awe. They were back at the fairy temple.

As soon as the effect of the blindness wore off completely, she looked around in more detail. She was at the base of the temple, staring up at the three majestic beings. They floated effortlessly a foot or so above the ground, staring down at her and Roki with blank expressions. The sound of Roki's heavy armor rattling around as he stood to his feet, reminded her that she was still kneeling over Dax's lifeless body. Leena looked down at her friend once again with great emotion. A familiar, yet unexpected, voice gave her a start as the head fairy spoke.

"Bring his body, quickly," she said, in a calm and mechanical manner. Leena looked over at Roki quickly. His face seemed to show reluctance, but he followed the order, hoisting Dax's body onto his broad shoulders. Roki walked forward, following the magical creatures as they hovered across the ground and into the temple. As they reached the dark inner room of the serene temple, the fairies turned and stopped beside the healing pool of blue water.

"Put him down into the water," The fairy ordered softly. Roki looked back at her a final time before stepping down into the pool. His body was strong, but it looked tired. Leena could see his shoulders bow as he carried Dax's limp body over one side. She could see the small stream of blood still flowing from his badly injured shoulder. As the water met Roki's waist, he lowered Dax's body slowly into the pool. He walked a few steps deeper and released his grip, letting his lifeless friend drop down underneath of the water. Leena stared uncomfortably as her friend's body disappeared beneath the blue surface.

The fairy nodded towards the pool, motioning her to go in as well. Leena looked at the cool blue water. Her rigid body ached with pain. The water seemed to draw her towards it. She remembered the last time, how soothing the cool water had been. She didn't question it further as she walked forward and took a step into the pool. The swirling blue water seemed to penetrate her boot instantly without drenching it. But she still had so many questions. She turned back towards the magnificent beings with a curious expression.

"Why...?" she started. But before she could ask her question the fairy interjected.

"We will speak soon enough, hero. Relax now and heal."

Leena let her questions drift to the back of her mind as she turned back to the pool. It could wait. Somehow, she knew her questions would be answered shortly. Her body relaxed as she let herself descend into the cool blue water. Her heavy body sank down quickly below the surface, allowing the swirling water to rush all around her. As her head sank deeper, she could just make out Dax's familiar shape somewhere near the bottom as beams of light weaved back and forth around his body. Her eyes were heavy. She closed them and relaxed her mind as the water seemed to carry her quickly, as if her body was rushing downstream. The feeling was invigorating. She didn't resist as it grew dark and quiet. It was peaceful. Within seconds, she was asleep, sinking ever deeper into the dark silence.

Cold air rushed into her lungs as Leena sat up quickly and looked around. Her heart beat rapidly in her chest as she glanced around the dark temple. Where was Roki? Leena stood to her feet and instantly noticed the lack of pain in her body. It felt great, like her wounds had never happened. She turned around and started toward the entrance when she spotted Roki's familiar shape across from her on the other side of the pool.

He sat on the floor with his feet crossed, staring down at Dax's body that lay next to him. Her heart dropped into her stomach again as the sight of her fallen friend returned. Somewhere deep down she had hoped it was all just a bad dream. She walked over slowly and placed her hand on Roki's shoulder. He looked up at her with a smile on his face, before nodding at Dax's body. Leena looked down at Dax, trying to figure out what Roki was smiling about. She didn't see anything worth feeling happy about. Then she caught it. It was the faint motion of Dax's chest moving up and down as he breathed. She couldn't believe her eyes. Dax was alive.

Leena looked up and smiled at Roki as she wiped the happy tears from her eyes. "I can't believe it," she choked, fighting back more tears. "I thought I had lost him…" She let her words fade as she fought to hide her feelings from him. Roki looked at her with passionate, knowing eyes. "Leena, It's okay. You two are my best friends, nothing will ever change that. I will always be here for you." He reached in and hugged her tight as she sobbed happily into his shoulder.

She sat there motionless in the inner temple for a few minutes, enjoying the calming atmosphere. It had been quite a journey. They were all together, and most importantly, alive. She couldn't wait to get back to Meadow Haven and put the whole experience behind her.

Suddenly she jumped as Dax's unexpected movement startled her. He sat up quickly with a gasp. She watched his right hand grab at where his previously-fatal wound had been. Then he looked around frantically, trying to make sense of what was going on.

"What happened?" Dax questioned nervously. "Everything went dark..."

She leaned in and put her hand on Dax's arm. "We thought we had lost you," she said, fighting back a few more tears.

"If the fairies hadn't brought you here when they did..." Dax reached forward and hugged her tightly. His passionate embrace caused a flood of mixed emotions.

"Don't cry," he whispered in her ear, before leaning back and looking into her eyes. "You're not going to get rid of me that easy," she smiled through watery eyes as Roki let out a small chuckle.

"Well, if you would learn how to fight!" he quipped. Dax smiled back at him.

"So, what of the dark creature?" Dax questioned. Roki turned and looked at her with a respectful expression.

"We defeated him, thanks to Leena. Her arrow saved us all," Roki answered.

Suddenly Leena saw a flash of white light and the fairies were present once more.

"You have done well, heroes," the head fairy spoke.

"You have vanquished a powerful foe. But we are afraid the true darkness behind this has not been stopped. We can still feel his wicked powers growing stronger. We fear that the risen mage king was merely a servant, drawing his power from a more sinister master."

Leena glanced at her two friends with unbelief. She couldn't believe that the vile creature that had nearly claimed their lives had only been a mere pawn. What kind of dark being could be more powerful than what they had faced? Who could stop a foe such as that?

"We have more to discuss with you, but that time is not yet. We will learn more of this darkness. It is time for you to return home and rest. You have earned your leisure," the fairy said, as the three of them stood to their feet. "We will open a path for you to return home."

With a loud cry, the three magnificent beings faded into swirls of bright light as a new path opened in the trees. The magical pool had healed Leena's wounds, but her body still felt tired as she walked forward towards the opening. She couldn't believe that they had survived it all. They had come so close to failure, and so many strange things had happened. It had been quite an adventure, but she was glad that it was over.

As Leena walked towards the opening in the trees, she glanced over at her friends. Roki looked sturdy as he walked next to Dax, helping him to support his still weakened body. He was a good friend. They were lucky to have him.

Her eyes soon drifted to Dax. He walked along slowly, leaning on Roki for support. His perfect, orange hair was still spiked forward, as though it had never been touched. His dark brown eyes seemed softer and more focused than she had ever seen them. She could tell that their last battle had changed him somehow. She felt a deep pain in her heart as she thought about how she had almost lost him. It was the most terrifying feeling she had ever experienced. She never wanted to feel it again. No matter how much she had to train, she would make sure that she would never fail to protect him again. As Dax's soft brown eyes met hers, she finally realized the truth. She was in love.

Chapter XVIII

Once they exited the secret forest temple, the lush serene forest welcomed them once again. Dax took in a deep breath of the fresh cool air. His lungs immediately picked up all the subtle scents that he had come to love from their many past adventures.

The forest seemed especially calm and serene, like its peace had been restored. He couldn't help but feel happy as he looked out over the gentle scenery. They had done it. They had vanquished the dark force that held the forest in its clutches. They had overcome their greatest challenge. The forest he loved, the town he loved, and the people he loved were safe, at least for the time being. Though, he knew it wasn't his own doing. He had failed in his duty as leader. He was supposed to be able to protect his friends. But, he had failed. If it wasn't for Leena, none of them would be alive. It was an odd mix of emotions, his admiration and affection for Leena tempered with the shame of his own failures. Even though he was at peace with the outcome, he knew he had to get better. He could never allow himself to fail like that again. He was the leader, and it was time for him to start acting like one.

ABOUT THE AUTHOR

David A. Brogdon writes mystical tales of fantasy and adventure, taking place anywhere from medieval-style kingdoms to post-apocalyptic future. He enjoys bringing to life beautiful landscapes, memorable characters, and epic adventures.

The Dark Forest is his debut novel. With it, he desired to create an engaging tale that would be easily approachable for young readers, while also paying homage to classic fantasy and role playing such as D&D. It blends heavy action and adventure, packed with nostalgic heroism, colossal battles, and just a little bit of romance to create a truly fun experience that can be enjoyed by fantasy lovers of all kinds.

David was born in Red Bluff, California and lives in rural Arkansas with wife and three children. He has multiple novels in the works. Visit learningtowrite87.blogspot.com for more info!